*The Five Million
Dollar Prince*

The Five Million Dollar Prince

MICHAEL BUTTERWORTH

PUBLISHED FOR THE CRIME CLUB BY

DOUBLEDAY & COMPANY, INC.

GARDEN CITY, NEW YORK

1986

All of the characters in this book
are fictitious, and any resemblance
to actual persons, living or dead,
is purely coincidental.

Library of Congress Cataloging-in-Publication Data

Butterworth, Michael, 1924–
The five million dollar prince.

I. Title
PR6052.U9F58   1986   823′.914   85–46077
ISBN 0-385-23542-9

Tour 3

. . . should include the ALBERT HALL (q.v.) and, most particularly, the PRINCE ALBERT NATIONAL MEMORIAL, which much-maligned example of mid-Victorian Art and Architecture in their apogee soars to a height of 180 feet on a commanding site in Kensington Gardens.

Designed by Sir George Gilbert Scott, the monument was completed in 1872, and the statue of PRINCE ALBERT by John Henry Foley, R.A., was added in 1876.

The cost of the whole was £120,000.

—from *The Modern Tourists' Rational Guide to London* (Marlowe, 1985)

The Five Million Dollar Prince

ONE

"All out, ladies and gentlemen—please."

Bunbury intoned the request in his well-honed, Oxford-accented baritone, and allowed his charges to file out of the coach and into the sudden sunlight of the parking space at the side of the Albert Hall, he remaining seated; this afforded him the opportunity to make a wistful appraisal of one or two of the more attractive younger females in his party and also—more important—to take a hefty slug from the silver-plated hip-flask (a relic of happier and more prosperous days) in the surreptitious manner that he believed—quite mistakenly—to have escaped the notice of the members of Scott & Lloyds Tour Party Number 12. They had noticed Horace Bunbury's drinking, all right. And much else about him. In fact, it was only his strident accent allied to an air of cultured assurance that had prevented the thirty-six United States citizens of Tour Party Number 12 from coming out in open rebellion against the drunken creature with the unkempt beard who insisted upon wearing a shabby overcoat, pullover, and woolly scarf in the height of a heat wave, and who fell asleep, mouth agape and snoring stertorously, whenever the coach was on the move.

"Where now?" A blue-rinsed matron with steely eyes that had lit quite often upon the unprepossessing tour guide, and always with disfavour, delivered the demand as Bunbury alighted unsteadily from the coach.

"To the Albert Memorial, ma'am," he responded, pointing to the spired monolith that reared, tier upon tier, from a grassy knoll beyond the bustling traffic of Kensington Gore.

"Can't we photograph it from *here?*" demanded Steely-eyes, with the air of one who delivers a great truth. "I, for one, have a telephoto lens, so why do I need to go up close?"

"The monument, ma'am," intoned Bunbury, rocking back slightly on his heels. *"That* monument, erected by the love of a queen and the gratitude of her people, well repays a closer look.

"This way, please, ladies and gentlemen."

Kensington Gore around noon on a Saturday is no place for jay-walkers, but Bunbury, ignoring a perfectly good pedestrian crossing twenty yards further along, marched boldly out into the traffic, both hands raised to deter any driver of homicidal intent. The sheer effrontery and unexpectedness of his action carried the day: the traffic stopped, and, like Moses of old, Bunbury led his flock safely between the parted sea of frustrated vehicles.

They came to the looming monolith, and the camera shutters began to clack-clack; above the racket there rose the cultured voice of the tour guide.

"The colossal statue of Prince Albert is placed beneath the vast tabernacle, surrounded, as you see, by the works of sculpture illustrating the arts and sciences which His Royal Highness fostered.

"The Prince, as you will observe, is seated. There was earlier a move afoot to represent him in a kneeling posture—as at prayer—but this was deemed to be an undignified pose for a royal personage.

"Will you kindly move along this way, please. . . ."

Passing down one side of the vast, square base of the monument, the party presently came to a sculpted group set high on a plinth: a companion piece to those set at the other three corners of the edifice. The heroic-sized figures were of nonspecific aboriginal appearance and the central, female figure (she was mounted upon a buffalo) was exposing one voluptuous breast—an artistic convention of the Victorian period which was strictly adhered to throughout the edifice.

"Be-yootiful—be-yootiful!" The comment came from the personage standing closest to Bunbury: a smallish, stout man in a lightweight suit, bootlace tie, and a white cowboy hat. The former had had some small exchanges with the other and had found him most agreeable in manner; George G. Sawtry by name, and a Texan.

"Quite so," agreed Bunbury. "What we have here, ladies and gentlemen, is one of a group of four sculpted tableaux in the round, each representing one of the four major continents.

"*America* herself is personified by the Indian woman . . ."

"Be-yootiful—be-yootiful!" intoned Mr. George G. Sawtry.

". . . mounted on a buffalo and charging through the long prairie grass. Her advance is directed by the figure representing the United States on one side, while, on the other, Canada attends her, pressing the Rose of England to her breast.

"In the other figures of the composition are presented Mexico, with a somewhat Aztec face, rising from a trance of long ages; and also South America, in sombrero and poncho, equipped as for the chase.

"We proceed, ladies and gentlemen."

The sheer effrontery of the monument, its size, its richness of invention as regards the mixing of styles and proportions, and the cheerfully confident and overwhelming vulgarity of the monster mishmash subdued Scott & Lloyds Tour Party Number 12 to an awed silence—as it has done everyone since the day that Queen Victoria first launched this tribute to her beloved Albert upon an undiscerning world.

Silent they were—all save Mr. George G. Sawtry.

"Be-yootiful—be-*yootiful!*"

"Around the podium supporting the figure of the Prince and the tabernacle," resumed Bunbury, "are sculpted life-sized figures in high relief, representing the one hundred and seventy-eight men (there are no women) whom the Victorian Establishment considered to have most excelled throughout the ages in the arts of poetry, music, painting, architecture, and sculpture. Some of the names will strike a chord with you: Virgil, Shakespeare, Handel, Rembrandt, Palladio, Praxiteles, Bernini. . . .

"Some, however, amply demonstrate one's Victorian forebears' uncanny knack of backing losers. I mean—whoever heard of Grétry, Lawes, Thorpe, and Bupalus—not to mention Bird?"

The touch of levity won him a concert of titters from his captive audience, save from Steely-eyes and her immediate circle, while Mr. George G. Sawtry opined that it only confirmed his opinion of the supremacy of the male animal, goddamnit.

Progressing ever upwards, the party mounted the final raft of steps and stood before the podium, to gaze up into the austere and massive bronze countenance of Albert the Good.

"Habited in the robes and insignia of the Order of the Garter," said Bunbury, whose throat was getting dry and who craved for a long pull at the silver-plated flask of his delight that was burning a hole in his hip pocket. "And to identify the figure with one of the most memorable undertakings of the Prince's public life—the International Exhibition of 1851—a catalogue of the works collected in that first gathering of industry of all nations is placed in his right hand."

"The Prince must have been a man of great foresight, sir," declared Mr. George G. Sawtry. "An internationally orientated seer. The outstanding Englishman of his time."

"In fact, sir," responded Bunbury without embarrassment, "he was a German. Notwithstanding which, he was held in great regard by his adoptive country." He pointed upwards. "As one can read from the inscription that encircles the tabernacle." And he read it aloud:

> " 'Queen Victoria and her people
> to the Memory of Albert, Prince Consort,
> as a Tribute of Their Gratitude
> For a Life Devoted to the Public Good.' "

"Amen," said the Texan, who had removed his hat during Bunbury's reading and placed it over his left breast. "I tell you, sir, that I would give one helluva lot to own this edifice. Yes, sir —to take back this edifice and re-erect it on the edge of my parkland overlooking the range, I would give one helluva lot."

"Would you now?" commented Bunbury without interest. He thought he detected upon the other's breath the tang of spiritual blessing, and discerned that he was not the only one present who had imbibed heavily that forenoon. It takes one to know one.

"I would give, say, five million dollars," said Sawtry.

"That's a very great deal of money," said Bunbury, glancing at the other's ornate wrist-watch—his own had long since been bartered in exchange for drink—and blessing the thought that he would be parting company with Tour Party Number 12 for ever after he had deposited them at their hotel for luncheon.

George G. Sawtry stared at his companion in some surprise. "I have read in the tourist guide that this edifice cost one hundred and twenty thousand pounds when it was erected nigh on a hundred years ago," he said. "Taking into account the slide of world currency in the time between, I reckon that five million would be just about the right market price for today—having regard to wear and tear and general dilapidation that's taken place since."

If anything, thought Bunbury, the fellow's even drunker than I am.

"A real snip at the price," he commented ingratiatingly.

The return to the coach across Kensington Gore presenting the same problem as before, Horace Bunbury essayed to resolve it in a similar manner. He had tailed behind during the short walk from the monument to the edge of the main road which they must cross, and had imbibed deeply of the amber spirit in the hip-flask—consuming all the remainder of it in fact.

"Hadn't we best go by the pedestrian walkway?" suggested one of the more nervous members of the party, for whom the earlier re-enacted crossing of the Red Sea had been fairly traumatic.

Disregarding this effete proposal, Bunbury strode out into the road, one arm raised, holding in his other hand the expired hip-flask. And his party watched him go.

The car that struck him was bright red, sporty and snarly, and driven by a young sprig in a cheese-cutter cap and a cavalry moustache. The low-slung radiator grille took our hero at knee-level, careered him right over bonnet, windscreen, driver's seat, and tail-end, depositing him in an unconscious bundle of rags full in the path of a red double-decker London bus, the front offside wheel of which passed over the unfortunate tour guide's right leg at the knee joint.

Bunbury's treasured hip-flask, run over by the bus's front nearside wheel and split open at the joins, was sent flying into the gutter, where it was later swept up by a Council road cleaner, who, supposing that the twisted lump of antique Georgian silver plate was mere gun-metal, did not trouble to salvage it for himself, but tipped it straight into his tub.

Three months in the Royal Free Hospital allowed a small miracle to be performed on Bunbury's right knee joint, which was, with the aid of stainless-steel pins and a lot of expertise, restored to something like its former self, with the promise that its owner would suffer for the rest of his life from an "interesting" Byronic limp. His broken nose, shoulder-blade, tibia and fibula, and three ribs practically mended themselves.

The *via dolorosa* by which he was forcibly brought back from chronic alcoholism by far outstripped, in agony of body and mind, all the other misfortunes that had followed in train of his attempt to cross Kensington Gore on a Saturday rush-hour.

It began the morning after the accident—and he had recovered consciousness in the ambulance. He awoke with a habitual cough that brought on acute heartburn of the dyspeptic sort and caused him to have morning sickness—all symptoms that usually disappeared with his day's first five fingers' measure of whisky. Only—there was no morning's five-finger exercise on call at the Royal Free!

The young houseman who attended to him that first morning and helped prepare him for surgery was brutally sympathetic.

"Great opportunity for you—a dipso—to dry out," he said. "Why, you're going to feel so rotten from post-operative shock and all the rest of it that the withdrawal symptoms will fade into obscurity. Three days, four days—and you'll be a new man." He could not have been more wrong.

For four days and five nights, in and out of anaesthesia and post-operative shock, Bunbury suffered every inch of the stony path of the *via dolorosa* that leads away from chronic alcoholism: the hot and cold sweats, the shaking limbs, nausea, the shape of the whole body described in a sickening ache; the fine snowfalls that forever passed before the eyes, the noises in the head that with a little concentration could become voices —he knew them all.

By the time of his discharge, he had reached a healthy two hundred pounds in weight and was replacing the calorific content of anything up to a bottle and a half of whisky a day with chocolate bars washed down with innumerable five-finger measures of—soda water.

The social services people fitted him out with a reach-me-down suit, two sets of linen, and a pair of shoes, all second-hand. They also provided him with five pounds. Scott & Lloyds had sent him a letter of dismissal from their employ within days of his hospitalization, but this was only to be expected since, at the time of his accident, he had been retained only on sufferance, following numerous complaints from the clients about his drunkenness.

Bunbury's place of residence, and the repository of his few worldly goods, was an attic bed-sitting room in Pimlico. Returning there after his discharge from hospital, he found that the lock on his room had been changed. Enquiry of the resident landlord revealed that the accommodation had been re-let on account of his non-payment of rent for the period of his hospitalization and the month preceding. He departed from Pimlico homeless, his worldly possessions lumped in with his hand-out spare set of linen in a large plastic bag.

Bunbury's descent in the social scale had been gradual

enough for him not to have been made fully aware of the many benefits available to such as he in the modern welfare state. He had vaguely heard of something called the Department of Health and Social Security, representing a fount of perquisites innumerable, but finding the nearest office to be closed on Saturdays, and searching about for bed and board, he came upon the Norton House for Working Men—and enrolled himself there for a night's sleep with breakfast and a midday meal at the not outrageous charge of one pound and fifty pence.

The Norton House for Working Men was founded in the lean years of the 1930s by a philanthropic city alderman of that name. It differed from similar establishments by being non-denominational—indeed, non-religious—nor were the guests (and they were actually so designated) expected to perform menial housekeeping tasks in part-discharge of the reckoning; a man paid in hard coin of the realm and in return was provided with two meals of the coarsest fare and the hardest bed he was likely to endure in all his life.

Horace Bunbury was directed to dormitory 2 on the third floor, bed 23—the directions alone suggesting that he could not expect to enjoy the sort of privileged privacy that one might find at the Ritz Hotel or similar establishments. And so it was: bed 23 was half-way down a long room containing a score of others, and was set within touching distance of its neighbors; the bed situated on Bunbury's left was not made up, the right-hand one was occupied by a dark man in singlet and jockey shorts, apparently asleep, a gentle smile upon his sable-moustached lips.

Relieving himself of his worldly possessions, Bunbury flopped down upon the bed and rested his tired feet. This immediately won him the attention of his neighbour: one very dark blue eye flashed open, a question was posed.

"Did the bell go for luncheon—or have I slept through it?"

"I don't know," replied Bunbury. "I've only just arrived, but it's only barely midday. . . ."

"Then the mouldy bread will not yet have been sliced," declared the other. "Likewise the cheese, innocent still of the knife, remains a temple, whole and intact, for its writhing inmates. My name is O'Leary, Thomas O'Leary, late of the Irish Guards—how d'you do?" He extended a languid hand, which Bunbury took, and found to be warm, dry, and firm—like the touch of a snake.

"Horace Bunbury," he responded. "Sometime of Christ Church, Oxford."

"I had you at once for a man of education," said O'Leary. "Despite the broken nose."

"You have the looks of a soldier," said Bunbury. "Indeed, of a Guardee."

The compliments having been exchanged, the two fell to the probing out of each other: a trial passage of the cloak, a bit of picador work here and there—nothing too overt, nothing that suggested invasion of privacy. Very gentlemanly. Even allowing for O'Leary's unequivocal origins, very English. In the course of it, Bunbury gleaned what he had suspected: his companion came from right out of the top drawer of the Irish landed gentry, had been schooled in England, and had held the Queen's commission in the impossibly exclusive Guards' Division. In return for this intelligence, Bunbury let slip that his father, now deceased, had been a colonial administrator, that he himself had not taken a degree at Oxford, and that he was—and, surely, so much was obvious about them both—presently almost destitute.

"Then, since we have been brought together like this," said O'Leary, "children of misfortune both, we'll not lunch off bread and cheese today.

"Come on, Bunbury. Today we'll go Italian. Strictly on tick."

La Bella Ragazza in Dean Street, Soho, was no longer one of the most prestigious of Italian eating houses, and a stranger to the gourmet columns of the glossy magazines and top people's newspapers. So far as the two new acquaintances were concerned, however, the greeting accorded to O'Leary upon their entry held out the promise of certain advantages.

"Buon giorno, Capitano O'Leary. Your usual table, sí?"

Captain O'Leary's "usual table" was in a corner and provided a view of most of the other clients—an obvious plus.

"My credit's apparently still good here," observed Bunbury's host, "and this after eighteen months away. There's nothing to beat the snobbishness of your average Soho restaurateur, my dear Bunbury. I used to come here in the old days when it was the first of the trattorias to hit town and I was a debutantes' delight. Old Luigi, there, he would dearly love to call back the dear, dead days of his renown—with a little help from the likes of me." He grinned and added ruefully, "And I wouldn't mind going back to being a deb's delight again, either.

"What are you going to have?" Picking up the menu.

"I'll take my lead from you," said Bunbury.

In the event, and upon O'Leary's recommendation, they started with tortellini, pasta dumplings stuffed with chicken and ham, covered with a cream and Parmesan sauce.

"Very good—and very rich," observed O'Leary. "Speaking of which, I've been given a dead cert for the two-thirty race at Newbury, if only I could remember its name. Do you follow the gee-gees, Bunbury?"

"No, it's never been a weakness of mine," confessed the other.

O'Leary sent out for a newspaper, from which he gleaned that the filly in question—which, so his informant had assured him, stood as much chance of losing the two-thirty as a pork chop has of winning acclaim at a bar mitzvah—was named Tiresome Girl. He also lit upon another item—and this won his casual interest.

"Ha! I see that George G. Sawtry is fixing himself up with another wife," he observed. "His seventh—and predictably some years distanced from the sixth, and by the usual arithmetical progression—backwards."

"I knew a fellow by that name," said Bunbury. "He came from Texas and wanted to buy the Albert Memorial."

"One more time," said O'Leary. "Give it me again, one more time. Right through. Real slow . . ."

After a protracted inquisition, during which the tortellini had gone cold, it had come to this. . . .

"George Sawtry?" quizzed the Irishman.

"Yes."

"George *G.* Sawtry—you sure?"

"Positive."

"Texas?"

"Texas."

"Little fellow—face like a monkey?"

"You could say that—yes."

"This little fellow?" And for the first time, O'Leary produced the half-length photograph that was included in the newspaper text about the much-married George G. Sawtry.

"By Jove—yes, that's him all right—*my* George G. Sawtry!"

"And he's in the market to buy the Albert Memorial for five million dollars?"

Bunbury shifted uncomfortably in his seat. "Well, yes, he had some loose talk along those lines. Said that, by comparison with the original cost nearly a hundred years ago, it was a fair price. But—well, you know how it is—I figured that he'd had a drop and was just shooting his mouth off a little."

O'Leary folded his arms and gazed reflectively at his companion.

"Do you know—didn't you see in the papers the other week —what this guy is quoted as being worth in round figures?" he demanded.

Bunbury shook his head.

"Nobody knows," said the other. "But from the alimony figures to his six divorced wives, it's been estimated at over one hundred and twenty million dollars. And *that's* just liquidity. No one knows—no one will ever know—what Sawtry's hidden assets are, save that they'd make his liquidity look like peanuts."

"Great Scott!" cried Bunbury.

"Did you not know that this guy's predilection for collecting every kind of bric-à-brac from medieval castles to Japanese netsukes leaves the late William Randolph Hearst looking like a rummager among junk shops? Were you not around when he bid for the *Queen Mary,* and only withdrew his offer out of pique when it was clear that her present most gracious Majesty wouldn't be persuaded to perform the handing-over ceremony off his private stretch of coastline in Texas? Are you not cognizant with his offer to finance NASA with the means to take the executive committee of the Flat Earth Society on a cruise through space in order to squash the last remaining doubts of anyone on earth that our planet isn't a globe?

"Not only rich beyond the legendary dreams of avarice, my dear Bunbury, but this guy is also a nut and an eccentric of the purest water. And you say that, apart from your curious little encounter by the Albert Memorial, you've never heard of him!"

Bunbury spread his hands. "True," he admitted. "But then, I never so much as glance at newspapers and am dolefully ill informed on current affairs. Why, I couldn't name a single member of the present government—apart from the Prime Minister, of course."

O'Leary dabbed his lips, screwed up his napkin, and tossed it beside his only half-emptied plate.

"Well, so much for luncheon," he said. "Too bad—but we've much too much to do this afternoon.

"Luigi!" he called to the proprietor, who came running.

"Sí, Capitano?"

"My bill, Luigi."

"Sí, Capitano—subito."

The bill was produced. O'Leary was about to sign it when a thought appeared to strike him. "Do you know, Bunbury, I've only just realized that it's Saturday and the bank will be closed. Luigi, will you please be so good as to stick another tenner on the bill and give me the cash out of the till, there's a good chap."

Luigi was only too delighted further to ingratiate himself and his establishment with this ageing debutantes' delight—for what social advantages might not come of it?

They left the restaurant, the pair of them: half a meal and ten pounds to the good. "Better hurry," said O'Leary.

"Why?" asked Bunbury, puzzled.

"It's gone two-fifteen. Got to put this tenner on that filly's nose for the two-thirty. We need working money—and this is only for starters.

"Come on—*run!*"

Having always taken rather a dusty view of the Sport of Kings, Horace Bunbury lived in no great hopes of his new acquaintance's augmenting the tenner that he had abstracted from the restaurateur by what had looked very much like sharp practice. His surprise was only to be imagined, then, when the filly Tiresome Girl romped home first with no very great effort at the most attractive price of 15 to 1.

Thomas O'Leary winked at him as he stuffed the banknotes into his scuffed wallet, which was of crocodile skin, nevertheless.

"The next stop's rather a long traipse," he said. "We'd better take a cab. Got any money, Bunbury, old chap?"

Bunbury had the change from his social services fiver, after deduction of his one night's bed and board at Norton House. And said so.

"You pay for the cab," said O'Leary. "We're going to need every penny of this hundred and sixty.

"Here's a cab! He's seen us—*come on!*"

Seated in the taxi and driving south-east, Bunbury gave himself over to irritation at his companion's manner, not to mention the imperious way with which O'Leary had tacitly assumed that he had agreed to fall in with whatever plan had sprung alive and fully armed from the other's no doubt fertile Celtic brain.

"*Come on—come on*"—it was the Duchess from *Alice in*

Wonderland, all over again, with him, Bunbury, cast in the role of Alice!

And one had better tackle him about this present enterprise. . . .

"One thing puzzles me slightly," mused O'Leary, breaking in upon his companion's uneasy thoughts. "It's the question of why a guy like Sawtry should get himself mixed up in a two-bit rubbernecking tourist coach party, when he could have been chauffeured around in a Civil Service Rolls with some undersecretary of state from the Foreign Office giving him the red carpet tour."

Swift to defend his late status as tour guide, Bunbury responded with a tartness that had been stimulated by his present irritation. "I would point out that Scott & Lloyds deal only with Top People as clients," he said. "Likewise, all their tour guides are Oxbridge graduates"—he had the grace to stumble over this—"or *near*-graduates. I would add that the last London tour which I conducted numbered in the party the Dean of Vassar and—so I was confidentially informed—a prominent ringleader of the Mafia."

"Well, that answers my question," said O'Leary mildly.

"However," resumed Bunbury, who had got the bit between his teeth and was determined to put his mind to rest about a lot of things, "I should like to know why—"

"We're here," interjected O'Leary, who had been gazing out of the window at the passing scene of unlovely south London shopping streets. "Draw up alongside that jewellers' shop, cabbie," he called through the driver's partition.

Sulkily Bunbury paid off the cab (£2.60 plus tip) and followed his companion, who, to his surprise, was not entering the jewellers' by the front entrance, but was heading for a discreet door down a side alley, over which was limned the legend—meaningless to him:

PLEDGES*

The encounter that followed, which Bunbury watched and

* For the fortunately uninitiated, an explanation of the term is in order: *pledge n.* (a) Item given as security for honouring of contract, settlement of a debt,

listened to, was forever enshrined in his memory as yet another major revelation along the downward path he had taken during his descent in the social scale. He looked, and was astonished; he listened, and was appalled.

"Hello, Uncle, you're looking younger and handsomer than ever!" This remark, by O'Leary, was addressed to a wizened and elderly male person of such attenuated stature that scarcely more than a head and shoulders supporting an elongated face and a prominent nose bearing pebble glasses appeared over the edge of a mahogany counter that was polished smooth by time and generations of shiny elbows.

The Irishman's addressee leaned forward, the better to focus upon the newcomer. Presently the elongated countenance spread itself laterally into a grin of recognition.

"My life! Well, if it ain't the Capting!" he croaked. "How long you been out, Capting?"

"Since yesterday," replied O'Leary.

"Done all your time, did you?"

"Lost all my remission," replied O'Leary. "Made certain allegations concerning the chief screw's parentage. All regrettably true."

"Brixton, was that?"

"Yes."

"My boy Abie, he's in the Scrubs," said Uncle.

"I was never in the Scrubs," said O'Leary. "The food there is reputed to be good, and the visiting Catholic chaplain celebrates the Tridentine Mass on the quiet."

"My boy Abie they done for receiving," said Uncle.

"They say he daily anticipates excommunication."

"For a mere hundred and fifty pounds they should not have given my boy seven years."

"Rome, in my opinion, is all washed up. They've ditched the Latin and next will go the spells and smells. I give the Holy Father another ten years."

---

etc., and in hazard of forfeiture upon non-fulfilment. (b) The drinking of a toast, and offering of good health therein. (c) *An item put into pawn at a pawn shop* . . .

—Spalding's Concise Dictionary (1980)

"What's a hundred and fifty pounds of cocaine? It goes no-where nowadays—a week's supply in south-east London. For that, seven years! In her grave must be turning the boy's poor mother."

"Well, we can't spend all day in pleasant chit-chat," announced O'Leary, "for there's much to be done. Uncle, may I present my friend and colleague Bunbury. Bunbury, old fellow, this is Uncle—who's known in south-east London by no other sobriquet. The lightener of our darkness and the repository of our burdens."

"How do you do?" said Bunbury stiffly, extending a hand which the other took, after first wiping his own upon his waistcoat.

"Any friend of the Capting's is welcome here—at special rates," declared the pawnbroker.

"We've come to redeem my cabin trunk, Uncle," said O'Leary. "I trust you have honoured the pledge."

The old man spread his hands. "For you, Capting, the pledge would stand for so long as the gates of Brixton was closed upon you," he said. "At the usual rate of interest, less the half per cent for a good customer."

"Let the Rothschilds tremble!" declaimed O'Leary. "Bring forth the pledge, manipulator of world markets!"

"Always making with the smart one-line put-down, our friend," said the old pawnbroker in a loud aside to Bunbury, and departed grinning. He came back within minutes, trundling before him on a barrow an enormous cabin trunk that was scuffed and peeled with long service, and seemingly held together only by the exotic steamship and airline labels that were plastered all over it, many overlapping. They depicted logos and views from the jet age, as well as nostalgic evocations of a more relaxed era of travel: the Blue Train, the Orient Express, Nile steamships; Shanghai, Surabaya, and Samarkand, Persepolis and Panama.

"The keys, Capting!" And Uncle handed them to O'Leary with the grandiloquent air of one of Genghis Khan's satraps presenting the keys of a captured city to the leader of the Golden Horde.

There were no less than three locks, which being unfastened, the Irishman opened wide the trunk, to reveal on one side, a rack of gentleman's suitings, and on the other, a chest of drawers.

"Everything here a man-about-town requires," declared O'Leary, opening one of the drawers and taking out a pile of silk shirts, Charvet ties, club and old school ties, silk neckcloths of all patterns and hues. And a pair of black silk pyjamas.

"Suits for every occasion," he continued, and took from the rack a suave tuxedo and a lightweight sports jacket of West of England tweed, along with a more robust Donegal. There were also—and Bunbury noticed them particularly—a full-dress scarlet tunic with the buttons spaced in fours, together with blue "patrols" and mess dress, all bearing the insignia of a captain in the Irish Guards.

"Try this on, Bunbury," said O'Leary, holding out the pin-striped top half of a formal City suit.

The other slipped it on. It fitted as though it had been measured, cut, and hand-sewn upon him.

"That is going to save us considerable clothing overheads," observed O'Leary, "since we're both the same size."

Ten minutes later, they were in a cab and speeding back to Norton House through the empty afternoon streets, with O'Leary's cabin trunk securely strapped into the luggage space beside the driver.

O'Leary was counting his money. "Uncle charged me ninety-five quid to redeem the pledge," he said. "I didn't take out a big loan on the goods before I went inside—didn't need it, of course. How much have you got left now, Bunbury?"

Bunbury told him—rather severely.

"Total of sixty-five pounds and ninety pence," mused the other. "One is tempted to splash out and move into a clean, cheap hotel, but since we'll need to raise at least a couple of grand as working money for the next stage of the con, we might as well put up with Norton House a few more days.

"Think you can manage that?"

This being the first time in their acquaintance that he had had his opinion sought upon anything whatsoever, Bunbury was emboldened to extend the topic to embrace the whole issue of the thing they were supposed to be about—whatever *that* was. . . .

"O'Leary . . ." he began.

"Yes, my dear Bunbury?"

"This business of raising what you call 'working money'— first the bet on the horse race, and now two thousand you mention . . ."

"Yes—go on."

"Well, I mean to say—just what have you got in mind? What's behind all this—this 'con' you mentioned?"

O'Leary stared at him, and the rich blue Celtic eyes were quite without guile. "My dear fellow," he said, "haven't I made it clear entirely?"

"No—I'm afraid you haven't."

The other sat back in his seat with a smile. "Well," he said, "there's nothing simpler than to put things plain.

"We're after selling the Albert Memorial to George G. Sawtry for five million dollars."

"Wu—we? Did you say—*we* are?"

"That's right—I thought it was tacitly agreed between us."

"But—that would be criminal!"

"Yes," conceded the other. "But you wouldn't say no to a half share in five million quid for the pleasure of making an old man happy, would you now?"

Horace Bunbury searched within his heart and found a great truth awakening there.

"No!" he declared. "No—I wouldn't! Except that . . ."

"Except that what?"

"Well—who *owns* the Albert Memorial?"

"The English, I suppose. You, my dear fellow, must own

about one forty-sixth million part of the whole. Do you want to keep it?"

Bunbury thought of the monolith opposite the Albert Hall, dwelling particularly upon such aspects as the disproportion of figures; the cacophony of juxtaposed colours; the representation of Mexico "rising from a trance of long ages" (in the immortal words of the architect); the bathetic image of the great lumpen bronze Prince in his Garter robes and knee-breeches, holding the Great Exhibition catalogue of 1851. . . .

"No, I do not!" he cried, causing the taxi driver to start, swerve, and narrowly miss an oncoming bus. "I don't want to keep it at any price!"

TWO

Women and drink had brought about Horace Bunbury's downfall; to be fair to him, only one woman was directly involved; on the other hand, there was eventually a very great deal of drink.

In his heyday, while at Oxford and sweetening the delights of that idyllic existence with the help of his quite handsome patrimony, Bunbury was hard put to spend more than was needed to provide him with the lightweight social life of rowing and debating clubs, a modest wardrobe, occasional theatre trips up to London, and the odd half pint of beer with his best, and indeed only, Oxford friend, Mark Oyley. Bunbury was not a considerable socializer. Nor had he, at the age of twenty, any experience of the opposite sex in any sense whatsoever: his mother died in his infancy; he had been impounded in various one-sex boarding schools from the age of eight till nineteen; there were no female relations or friends; while his father, a retired colonial officer, had been a conscientious misogynist who, rather than employ a daily woman for the small, three-bedroomed house in Bath that he bought when his wife died, had put up with the sullen services of an ex-soldier named Peterson, who swept dust under carpets, carried on a clandestine relationship during working hours with the married woman next door, and cheated Bunbury senior with the housekeeping money.

After his father's death, when Horace had just gone up to Christ Church, he decided to keep on the Bath house and retain the services of the egregious Peterson—a decision that he later had cause to regret.

It was during the Michaelmas term of his second year that

he met Periwinkle Dawson, a barmaid who preferred to style herself a licensed victualler's assistant. Periwinkle, whose ambition was set on a higher plane than pulling half-pints in a saloon bar and accepting the light-hearted courting displays of penniless undergraduates, soon discerned that Horace Bunbury fitted her requirements in more than one area—and set her cap upon this financially secure and rather vague young man who scarcely seemed to regard her as other than a piece of furniture around the place.

To everyone's surprise—and none more so than Horace himself—the couple were soon engaged to be married, and Periwinkle spent the Christmas vacation with him at the tiny house in Bath. It was there that, almost upon entering the place, she came dangerously near to overplaying her hand by imperiously demanding a separate bedroom before Horace— to whom any other arrangement would never have occurred, upon so lofty a pedestal did he place his intended—had time to explain that she was having *his* room, and that he was moving up into the attic. The housekeeper Peterson, who had moved in permanently, occupied the only other decent bedroom on the same floor as that given over to Periwinkle; Horace would never have dreamed of shifting him out, for fear of offending him.

The sleeping arrangements suited everyone save Horace, who was kept awake over Christmas by a dripping water cistern in the attic. The woman next door was also aggrieved because Peterson neglected her over the holiday period.

In the New Year, Periwinkle brought the issue of marriage to a point by entering into negotiations for the purchase of a villa in Spain, her idea being that they would repair there after Horace had gained his degree, and that he would employ himself by writing best-selling novels. To this end, and to facilitate her arrangements, Horace made over a fairly large sum of money to his fiancée and further simplified their financial lives by putting his bank account in their joint names.

The marriage ceremony was fixed for the week preceding the groom's preliminary examinations in the Trinity term.

This was his own idea: he figured that he would have done all his revisions by then, and be inspired to success by the manifest blessings of Hymen.

Alas, for the blessings of Hymen . . .

In the long, empty months and the dreary years that followed, Horace Bunbury frequently looked back in anguish to that awful morning in the college chapel, when he had stood alone at the altar rail, with the Dean shuffling from one foot to another. No bride. No best man, either.

It transpired that Periwinkle and the best man, Mark Oyley —that snake in the grass!—had absconded, along with the Bunbury patrimony, and they were never seen again; the dream villa in Spain had existed only in estate agents' brochures.

With leadened tread, Horace betook himself in due course to the Examination Schools, where, after taking one jaundiced look at the paper, he retired to the nearest public house and downed three large whiskies—the first batch of many such.

Back in Bath on a quasi-permanent basis, he struck up a surprising rapport with Peterson, who, for a reason he disclosed only on his deathbed, was as desolated over the bolting of Periwinkle as his master had been. The ex-soldier took to the bottle—and Horace followed his example: nightly they drowned their sorrows in the distillation of the Highlands. Quite soon—in a matter of weeks—they were drinking right round the clock, neither party being able to face the rigours of the day spent staring at TV without the prop and support of the first five fingers of spirit upon rising.

After two years of this life, Peterson collapsed and was rushed to hospital, where he died a week later with Horace Bunbury holding the other's palsied hand in his own—but not before he had shattered the last of his employer and sometime drinking companion's illusions by confessing that he had several times enjoyed the delights that Periwinkle had denied her fiancé—commencing with the memorable Christmas.

The lost ten years of Horace Bunbury's life can be dated from immediately after Peterson's funeral and his abandonment of the little house in Bath, which had become unbearable to him because of the recurring image of Periwinkle enjoying the gnarled clutches of the old soldier.

He sold the house for a bad price and went to London to seek his fortune. Some excellent connections through his late father, the former colonial administrator, saw him through the first, and relatively prosperous, two years in the outer world. A sinecure was obtained for him in the Stock Exchange; but his taste for early morning drinking, resulting in his habit of taking naps on the floor of the 'Change during the most excitingly "bullish" times of the day, led the Chairman himself to suggest that he might well find his fortune more agreeably elsewhere. . . .

A short stint at Lloyd's was followed by an almost imperceptible lurch towards perdition when a distant cousin fixed him up with a seat on the board of a small insurance company that was occupied by the Official Receiver shortly after. Bunbury was not sent to prison with most of his fellow directors; but though innocent of any malpractice whatsoever, he was never again able to land himself a really prestigious job.

The descent of Bunbury then followed some fairly predictable steps. He became a "sales representative" for a firm of fancy goods purveyors by the simple means of answering a small advertisement, presenting himself at a warehouse in the East End, handing over ten pounds in exchange for a battered cardboard suitcase packed with flawed samples, and being sent out "on the road" to make his fortune at 2 per cent commission on all sales, no retainer or expenses, and a specific boundary—known as his "territory"—beyond which he must not stray. In just over two weeks, Bunbury was able to make only one sale worth mentioning: a substantial order of assorted knick-knacks from a small shopkeeper in Croydon, only to discover later that he had marginally stepped out of his territory to effect this *coup*, and into someone else's. The other sales representative, a former fair-ground boxer, was so incensed by Bunbury's piracy that he waylaid the other and hospitalized him for two months.

After salesmanship, Bunbury tried his hand at a sort of teaching. Offering his credentials as failed B.A. (Oxon.), wearing his most presentable suit, and displaying his unfailing good manners to the Principal of the Meecham Institute of Mental Development (Motto: *"No Man Is an Island—with a Developed Mind, He May Reach Out and Grasp the World for His Own"*), he was offered an appointment as Tutor and Scrutineer of the submissions made by corresponding students who had signed up for the course of twenty-four lessons which were more or less guaranteed to turn them into Einsteins or Rockefellers for a paltry fifty pounds down payment and six instalments of ten pounds.

The job suited Bunbury admirably. He put in a daily attendance at the "Institute" to pick up his quota of students' submissions and took them back to his lodgings over a fish and chip shop in Holborn, where he tussled with the recessive personalities, inferiority complexes, nervousnesses, inadequacies, and sensations of being about to be leapt upon from behind, from students as far afield as Manchester and the Scilly Isles, Devizes and Belfast. The going was greatly simplified by recourse to *Better Minds Without Tears* by J. V. Meecham, the bible of the Meecham Institute and the cornerstone of the method which had made old man Meecham a millionaire before he was forty. Aided by the good book, Bunbury dispensed pithy and trenchant responses to the students' submissions, his literary style and psychological insight greatly sharpened by the whisky glass that was forever at his elbow. By the age of thirty he had taken on the manner and appearance of an eccentric academic, with the beard, the disregard for sartorial appearance, unfailing good nature, and sweet manners. Two years later, his idyll crashed: the Meecham Institute went broke; he sank into a round-the-clock drinking habit that might have ended fatally, but for the intercession of an old schoolmate, who got him a job as tour guide with the highly prestigious Scott & Lloyds—with the results that have already been recorded.

Rosalind Purvis was a rather strait-laced young woman, the owner of a charming Georgian *cottage orné* in Kew which she shared with a vibrant brunette of her own age named Hannah McCracken, who worked in public relations. A graduate of the Courtauld Institute of Art, Ms. Purvis possessed a more than modest private fortune that enabled her to devote herself to voluntary work as secretary and treasurer of the Walbrook Trust, a charitable foundation set up by the trustees of the late Sir Aloysius Walbrook, Bart., soap manufacturer and lavish philanthropist, whereby indigent gentlefolk were, after perfunctory enquiries, provided with relatively generous financial assistance in paying for repairs and renovations to properties in their ownership that were deemed to be of genuine architectural and historical merit.

Such a claim for assistance, coming from a Major Denys Arbuthnot, M.C., of Wimbledon, and supported by letters from a notable Fellow of the Faculty of Architects and Surveyors and a prominent Associate of the Royal Institute of British Architects, together with an attestation from the Ancient Monuments and Historic Buildings Directorate of the Department of the Environment to the effect that the property in question was a Grade II Listed Building within the meaning of the Act, prompted Rosalind Purvis to write to Arbuthnot and fix an appointment to go and view the house and its roof, which was in need of partial replacement at the estimated cost of £6,000.

She drove herself to Wimbledon, and was received by Arbuthnot at the door of his charming Edwardian villa set in its own grounds not a stone's throw from the Mecca of international lawn tennis.

Arbuthnot led her into a sitting room that was furnished in the bachelor fashion with a plethora of school, university, and regimental group photos, inscribed rowing sculls, and the like —in addition to some delightful late Victorian and Edwardian pieces, and a strong William Morris influence in fabrics and wallpaper; notwithstanding which, Ms. Purvis noted tell-tale signs of genteel poverty: it showed in the much scuffed car-

pets, the lack of central heating, a general air of seediness. The
major himself, whose looks were dramatically heightened by a
broken nose and a romantic limp, was as smart as paint in a
pin-striped City suit and a Brigade of Guards tie; with his
dashing military moustache and straight-as-a-ramrod back, he
had the air of heroism lightly borne. Nevertheless, he had
frayed shirt cuffs.

He offered her tea—which she declined—and showed her
the estimate for the repairs, which were, hopefully, to be put
in hand by Messrs. Clegg & Sons of Balham. Mr. Clegg, Jr., said
Arbuthnot, was due at any moment, to explain the details of
the proposed repairs; and lo—Mr. Clegg, Jr., arrived dead on
cue.

Mr. Clegg was an engaging man about the same age as the
major. He was dressed in Donegal tweeds and had the easy
manner of an Irishman, though he did not speak with the
brogue, but with only a slight cadence that added an arresting
colour to his discourse. He took Ms. Purvis outside onto the
carriage drive and with his field-glasses directed her gaze to
the state of the roof. Six thousand, he said, was a good price
and the delay of as little as a twelvemonth must certainly
enhance it to seven or seven and a half, what with the rising
wages, cost of the materials, and so forth, doncher know? As to
terms: that would be one third down, one third half-way
through the job, and the balance on completion and entire
satisfaction.

His part in the transaction completed, Mr. Clegg, Jr., took
his leave. It was then, over a cup of tea in the sitting-room, that
Ms. Purvis was pleased to inform Major Arbuthnot that, yes,
the Walbrook Trust would offer two thirds of the cost of the
roof repairs, and £2,000 would be immediately available for
the initial charge.

The gallant major thanked her profusely and watched her
drive away down the road to the right. No sooner was her little
car out of sight than the Irishman reappeared from the left
and rejoined the "major."

"How did it go, then?" demanded the former.

"She fell for it—two thousand will be on its way this week!"

"Well done, we both!" said Thomas O'Leary, for it was he. He clapped Horace Bunbury on the shoulder. "You see how the combination of the blarney and the English smooth talk baffles intelligence. Even highly intelligent plain Janes like our Miss Purvis fall for it."

"Oh, I don't think she was all that plain," said Bunbury. "Quite attractive really, if she took stock of herself and did something about it."

"That's as may be," responded the other. "We'll leave Miss Purvis to her beauty problems. Right now we've the moving van coming from the junk shop to take back the loan furniture, and I've promised to return the keys to the estate agent before they close at half-past five. That being done, I'll take you and buy you a drink to celebrate our grafting the working capital for the big con on Sawtry."

"Oh, I keep forgetting you're on the wagon."

A week to the day that Thomas O'Leary had shaken the dust of Her Majesty's extraordinarily expensive, though unlavish, hospitality from his shoes, the gates of Her Majesty's prison, Wormwood Scrubs, London, W.12—known to fame and notoriety as "the Scrubs"—opened to a small group of dischargees, among whom one individual stood out from his former fellow inmates like a peacock surrounded by bedraggled crows; Lucifer in hell, light amidst darkness. From the crown of his curly-brimmed Homburg hat to the soles of his hand-made St. James's Street shoes, taking in the Savile Row covert coat, the Jermyn Street shirt and tie, and the Bond Street jewellery on the way, he was the very epitome of expensive overdressing, of ostentation on the dear. Big as he was—well over six feet and burly with it—he gave the impression of there being an even bigger man inside. His aquiline, imperious profile was of the sort that gladiators saluted before dying. The only disparate item was his voice: when he called out to the silver Rolls-Royce that was kerb-cruising nearby, it was curiously high-

pitched, reedy, almost effeminate—and irremediably East
End.

"Wake up, you lot! Wotcher—blind or somefing? Wotcher
fink I'm standing 'ere for?"

The sight and sound of him brought the Roller swiftly to a
halt close by, and two men leapt out, one to open the passenger door, the other to hand the released prisoner into the
limousine. The latter's former fellow inmates stood and
watched him depart in wistful silence, and then themselves
went their solitary ways, clutching their worldly possessions in
paper bags and battered attaché cases.

In the Roller, the big man sat between two aides; two more
were in the front, one driving.

The fellow on the big man's right—he who had helped him
into the vehicle—was lithe and ratty-looking. He on the left
side was dressed all in black, with black jowls that would not be
tamed by any razor. These two were known to the underworld
and the law as Weasel Jilkes and Darkie Todd respectively.
Their boss's name was lovingly limned in the police dossiers of
the United Kingdom as Cuthbert Judd, alias "the Man." The
two characters in the front seats were small-timers who both
answered to "you."

"Where to, boss?" asked the Weasel.

The question brought no response.

"Round to the club for a drink? It's just a suggestion." Silence denoting consent, he nudged the driver. "Take us to the
club."

"While you was in college, boss, Marie ran off with a drummer," said Weasel. "I told Darkie to write you, but he chick-
ened out."

"So what—I brung her back, din' I?" whined the latter. "An'
that drummer, I marked him good. He won't drum no more."

"He marked Marie, too," said Weasel. "Like we figured you
never take back a bird who's run off. She works in the club
kitchen now."

No comment from the Man.

"The Space Wars collections is up again, boss," said Weasel.

"Fifteen grand a week. Likewise the pool tables. New guy who moved into the Free Crowns pub, he frew out the table an' told us to get stuffed. We leaned on his kid. The table's back now."

The Man shifted in his seat. His dark eyes, smouldering under shaggy black brows like damped-down fires about to burst into incandescence, scanned the streets they passed along, totally ignoring his companions.

"Bonzo Skerritt and his mob, they're making trouble in the strip joints, boss. Last week they bid up the hush-money we pay out to that bent inspector, an' he closed us down in two places. I put the word out to croak Skerritt. I hope as how I did the right fing. . . ."

Weasel Jilkes's litany on the latest doings connected with the Man's multifarious business interests elicited not a flicker of interest from the latter—but he still persevered.

"Bernie Silver, he set up a joy house in opposition round the corner from Maggie's place, boss. But we spread the tale that his birds was all into herpes. Tuesday, Bernie closed down."

Darkie chipped in his piece. "Saturday, I wuz up in Newmarket," he whined. "Had a drink wiv this apprentice jockey what looked like he might be co-operative. Told him I'd had this bad dream about his poor old ma fallin' under a bus on her way to collect her pension. He'll be very happy to pull the fird race at Lansdown on Friday."

The one-sided conversation languished and died. They drove on in silence for a while, till the Roller was very near to the all-day-and-night drinking club in Whitechapel of which the Man owned the biggest piece of the action.

It was then that the damped-down fires that had been fighting for expression ever since he had entered the limousine burst to life in the Man's brain.

"That toffee-nosed Irish bastard!" he piped in the reedy, androgynous voice so ill suited to his fearsome looks. "That O'Leary! This town ain't big enough for the two of us!

"After what he done to me, that O'Leary's gotta go!"

The certain promise of a grant from the Walbrook Trust decided O'Leary and Bunbury to exchange the rigours of Norton House for a cheap but comfortable commercial hotel in Sussex Gardens, where such establishments seem to proliferate, presumably because of the proximity to Paddington Station, railway terminus for the West of England and for Wales. The owner of the Gwynedd Hotel, a Welshman named Arfon Jones-Evans, had scarcely ventured more than a couple of hundred yards from his destination before sinking his roots in the above-mentioned establishment, along with his wife, Blodwen, and his frighteningly nubile daughter, Myfanwy, who quickly set her cap on Thomas O'Leary, greatly fancying the exceedingly dashing military manner he had with him, and perhaps also succumbing to the call of Celt for Celt; in any event, she was forever waylaying him in odd holes and corners of the hotel, and mostly in a state of blushing *déshabillé*, as when emerging quite by chance from the bathroom in her shortie dressing-gown.

The two conspirators had taken a large double room on the second floor back, with ample accommodation for O'Leary's massive cabin trunk. Bunbury had been introduced to the manifest advantages of the trunk, which far exceeded the accommodation of gentleman's clothing. There was, for instance, a well-stocked cocktail bar secreted in one of the drawers (though this was, of course, of no interest to the newly enlightened teetotaller); a short-wave transmitter-receiver in another; and a miniature, but exceedingly efficient, typesetting and printing complex in the third. It was by means of the latter advantage that O'Leary had been able to set up and print the various authentic-looking letterheads that had so convincingly gulled Ms. Rosalind Purvis of the Walbrook Trust.

It was on the morning of Cuthbert Judd alias the Man's discharge from the Scrubs that the two of them held a council of war around the cabin trunk, which was opened to disclose the drawer—also open—containing what could only be described as the printing works. They had talked far into the previous night and hammered out a method of approaching

George G. Sawtry, now known to be staying at the Ritz Hotel, following upon his marriage to his seventh wife, one Desirée Hofmayer, a reputed socialite, late of Philadelphia, Pa.; contingent upon which O'Leary had burnt a fair amount of midnight oil in fleshing out the bare bones of their deliberations in a letter—more nearly a prospectus—which he handed to his accomplice for his comment. The missive bore an impeccably printed letterhead and was faultlessly typed upon the thickest and most expensive of papers.

George G. Sawtry, Esq.	CROWN AGENTS FOR OVERSEA
The Ritz Hotel,	GOVERNMENTS & ADMINISTRATIONS
Piccadilly,	4 Millbank, London, S.W.1
London, W.1.	Tel: (01) 222 7730
	Date as per postmark.

Sir,

Acting in accordance with our brief as financial, commercial, and professional agents for almost 100 governments and over 300 public authorities and international organizations, our services being available to any government and to any organization in the public sector, we the above agency have been empowered by the Ancient Monuments and Historic Buildings Directorate of the Department of the Environment to negotiate the sale and disposal of the Albert Memorial, at present situated in the Royal Kensington Gardens, London, S.W.7.

To this end, we propose to offer the monument for sale by private auction in the Runnymede Room of the Plantagenet Hotel, Knightsbridge, on the 29th of this month.

Private invitations to the auction are limited to eminent international collectors, and your name, sir, has been recommended to us for inclusion in the distinguished guest list.

In view of the sensational publicity which the sale would almost certainly attract from less responsible sectors of the media, we have determined, in the interests of our esteemed invitees, who include the gracious presence of Royalty, to treat the matter as confidential to all but the participants.

To this end, and to reduce revealing correspondence to a minimum, a senior member of the Agency will telephone you personally at an early opportunity and hopefully receive your acceptance verbatim.

For your kind attention, sir, a schedule of the event is appended herewith.

Yours faithfully,

[An illegible signature]
Chairman

The schedule was typed on a separate sheet:

PRIVATE AUCTION AND RECEPTION

Runnymede Room, the Plantagenet Hotel,
Knightsbridge, S.W.7

7:30 P.M.	Informal Reception
7:45 P.M.	THE QUEEN
8:15 P.M.	The Auction
8:30 P.M.	Buffet Supper
9:30 P.M.	Entertainment & Dancing
1:30 A.M.	Carriages

Bunbury having greeted his partner's presentation with acclaim, the letter was duly conveyed to the Ritz Hotel by hand of uniformed messenger hired from one of the agencies. It was delivered by page-boy to the suite of the Texan multimillionaire while the latter was breakfasting off ham, eggs, and flapjacks with maple syrup, plus his own blend of coffee that he took everywhere on his travels. His new lady wife was enjoying her more austere fare of unsweetened orange juice, whole wheat germ biscuit, and de-caffeinated coffee while sitting up in her Louis XV bed.

George G. Sawtry read the communication right through and gave a low whistle of amazement.

"Well, I'll be doggoned!" he exclaimed.

His bride winced to hear this homely expletive and fixed her spouse with a gold lorgnette that she wore on a fine chain about her alabaster neck; though only twenty-three—or so she claimed on her marriage certificate—the self-declared ex-debutante was generally described by her contemporaries as being piss-elegant to an excruciating degree.

"Why do you say this, George?" she asked.

"If this ain't a coincidence to beat 'em all," responded he. "When I tell you, hon, that the last time I was in London, I chanced to price a certain piece of real estate with no real hope of the same coming my way, and now, god-damnit, I have this letter to say it's up for grabs. This beats all—yes sir!"

He passed the letter and its enclosure over to his bride, who took it between her expensively manicured fingers and examined the same through her lorgnette.

"Baby, you are so goddamned refined," said Sawtry, struck with a sudden surge of admiration for his tender new acquisition. "The Queen of England herself ain't so goddamned refined as you, I bet!"

"Don't be coarse, George," responded she, shaking off his importuning hand, "you're mussing my night-gown." She re-addressed herself to the missive and presently laid it down.

"So what?" she demanded. "So who wants the Albert Memorial—whatever *that* is?"

"Desirée—Desirée!" George G. Sawtry's whole being was immediately bent towards introducing his bride to the demonstrable virtues of the edifice in question, and the desirability of possessing the same at almost any price: he told of the legacy of a great queen's undying love and that of her far-flung peoples, of the staggering artistic and architectural merits of the memorial, the enormous prestige that would accrue from the possession of same—particularly in that enclave of Texas where every citizen one brushes past on the sidewalk is either a millionaire or a multimillionaire, and the only thing that lifts one out of the common moneyed ruck is the possession of bigger, better, and more imaginative hardware.

Desirée listened to all this with admirable patience, but was not impressed. She was not impressed till he touched upon the Royalty who were to be present at the Plantagenet Hotel. This caused her to re-examine the letter and its schedule, where she indeed confirmed the truth of his assertion.

It was there in black and white: 7:45 P.M.—the Queen.

"George, you will take me to this affair," she declaimed imperiously. "And whether you buy the Albert Memorial or not is up to you."

"That's my gal!" cooed Sawtry, embracing her.

"Don't pull me around, George!" snapped his new bride. "You know it always brings on one of my morning headaches!"

Though deficient in many of the refinements to which the seventh Mrs. George G. Sawtry clove so passionately, the multimillionaire was far from being a sitting duck when it came to being put upon by people after his money. Later, dressed, barbered, and reeking of his favourite after-shave, put up exclusively for him by a top United States male cosmetician and called *Old Chaps*, he summoned his lifelong friend, former fellow cowpuncher, and present major-domo-cum-body-guard, Tex Manacle by name.

Tex entered his employer's dressing-room as if he were elbowing his way through the swing doors of a frontier bar, with a pair of phantom six-shooters never far from his muscular fingertips. A man of precisely Sawtry's age, which was sixty-two, he affected—and wore, indoor and out and at all times—not the kind of neat white Stetson favoured by contemporary men of the West, but the genuine antique article of his boyhood: the tall-crowned ten-gallon variety immortalized by Tom Mix, Ken Maynard, and other stars of the early Westerns. With this, he also affected a skin-fitting striped suit which revealed every rippling muscle of his six-foot five-inch frame —and permitted the avoirdupois at his midriff to hang over his studded waist-belt.

Expertly aiming a jet of tobacco juice into a vase of bronze chrysanthemums standing upon a Chinese lacquered table, Tex addressed his employer.

"What goes, Eagle-eye?" This was the sobriquet that Sawtry had earned for himself by spotting card-sharpers during innu-

merable stud poker sessions in the bunk-houses uncounted of
their youth.

"Tex, I want for you to check out a limey set-up that calls
itself the Crown Agents for Oversea Governments, etc., etc.
The address is right here. They may be on the level, they may
be phoney as hell. Just check 'em out. No rough stuff. Remember this is London. Okay. Take the boys in case there's any
trouble—but don't look for trouble. Check?"

"Check!" growled Tex. "What you doin' today, Eagle-eye?"

"I'm takin' the little woman shopping in Bond Street, which
is only just across the road a piece," replied the other, "so we'll
not be needing you. If I'm not around when you get back from
checking out these Crown Agent guys, leave a note with your
report at reception, willya?"

"Sure thing, Eagle-eye." Tex Manacle hitched up his waist-
belt, set his ten-gallon hat more firmly on his bullet head, and
strode out into the sudden sunlight of the Wild West.

By a circuitous routing, which involved in the first instance
an impeccably respectable, discreet, and outrageously expensive accommodation address in Ebury Street, there arrived
that day by the second post an envelope addressed to Major
Denys Arbuthnot, M.C., containing a short note addressed
from the Walbrook Trust stating that the latter had much
pleasure in enclosing their cheque for £2,000, being the first
instalment of the agreed sum of £4,000, which would be the
Trust's contribution to the restoring of Major Arbuthnot's roof,
etc., etc.—and signed in Rosalind Purvis's careful italic hand.

Bunbury regarded the cheque first with elation, and then, as
the image of Ms. Purvis's trusting, bespectacled countenance
supervened, with a leaden sense of guilt that he should have
been a party to deceiving and despoiling her virginal faith in
the honour and probity of the officer class; this was succeeded
by a switch of the mind not unconnected with the thought of a
half share in five million pounds, and he realized that
Rosalind's decision to stake Major Arbuthnot might be called
an investment. Yes—that was it! When he came into his two

and a half million, he would return the two thousand—anony-
mously, of course—together with interest at the current bank
rate plus.

His conscience mollified, he ran, rejoicing, to show the
cheque to O'Leary, and together they took it round and deposited it at the High Street bank where Bunbury had opened a
modest account with the few pounds left over from the first
tranche of their "working money."

THREE

Towards noon, Mr. and Mrs. George G. Sawtry strolled across Piccadilly in the glorious summer sunshine and wended their way down Bond Street, which shares with Fifth Avenue and the rue de la Paix the very condensation of all that is beautiful, elegant, and expensive in the Western world. After them, crawling along at strolling pace, came a chauffeur-driven Bentley, to pick up the lucky couple should fatigue overcome them in their travels.

The object of their outing—to buy a suitable wedding present for Desirée—was not quite so quaint as it sounds; for it happened that the couple had been married for only one week and had known each other for a week plus the three days it had taken to get a license; the issue of a present had simply not had time to arise.

Bond Street offering, as it does, the choice of nearly everything that is desirable under the sun in the way of portable goods, the range was immense; all things being equal, however, jewellery of some kind suggested itself as the prime option. Accordingly, the happy couple entered a famous emporium whose branches grace the capitals of Europe and the Americas, and demanded to be shown the best there was on offer.

Shrewdly sizing up the quality of their customers (and marking the Bentley parked outside their plate-glass doors—despite the importunities of a traffic warden, who was unable to dent the resolve of the chauffeur to remain right where he was), the underlings summoned the manager of the emporium himself to attend the little man in the Stetson and silk suit and his ravishing young companion.

At the manager's command, costly items of adornment were produced. They began with rings: diamond, ruby, emerald, and sapphire rings for choice, plus variations of the four stones mixed: Mrs. Sawtry the Seventh would have none of them. They progressed to collars, chokers, and necklaces, made up of the same primary stones with the addition of pearls. Desirée was half tempted by a choker comprising four bands of matched pearls worn high at the throat, Edwardian style, from which were suspended roped pearls of diminishing sizes, terminating in a pear-shaped diamond pendant around bosom level: her husband was already groping for his credit card when she changed her mind.

From there they progressed to tiaras, anklets, parures of all combinations—all to no use. Desirée, faced with *embarras de richesses et de choix,* simply could not make up her mind. They were bowed out of the emporium by the frock-coated manager with nothing but smiles.

It was the same with fine pictures. In and out of the smartest galleries, they viewed Rowlandsons and Hockneys, Dufys and Gainsboroughs, beach scenes by Boudin, nudes by Russell Flint: nothing would bring the glint of acquisitiveness to madame's eyes of cornflower blue.

Finally—almost despairing—George G. Sawtry had one of those brainwaves which had ordained that he became a multimillionaire whilst the sidekick of his youth, Tex Manacle, still remained basically a cowpoke.

"I'm taking you for a mystery tour, hon," he told her, and signalled to the following Bentley to pick them up.

Despite her entreaties, growing ever more irritable as they progressed westwards along Piccadilly, Knightsbridge, and Kensington Gore, her grinning spouse would not divulge their destination, and by the time the circular mass of the Royal Albert Hall hove into sight like some gigantic fruit-cake, madame was having the sulks.

Telling the chauffeur to stop right there, Sawtry then took his wife's hand and, helping her to alight, led her across Kensington Gore (by way of the pedestrian crossing) and towards the looming spire of the tabernacle that housed the bronze representation of Albert the Good.

Brought up close to the soaring monument in all its triumphant vulgarity, Desirée could only watch, wonder, and enthuse.

"Why, Georgie—it's—it's wonderful! . . . What *is* it?"

"It's yours, hon—your wedding present!"

He kissed her in the shadow of the lowering memorial, and a crocodile of little schoolgirls tittered and nudged each other as they filed past, two by two, with a manifestly disapproving nun at their head.

And Desirée did not complain about his mussing her make-up—for once.

They had luncheon at a gourmet establishment off the Brompton Road that was recommended by their chauffeur, who was up to date with all the trends and took his cut from the management.

Arriving back at the Ritz in time for tea, Sawtry was handed an envelope by the clerk at reception. It was addressed to him in the fine sprawling hand of his trusted aide Tex Manacle. He read it at tea—in between casting covert and adoring glances at his young wife, who had changed into a hostess gown for the ritual of presiding over her tea trolly with its Darjeeling and its Rose Congou infused in silver pots and the copper kettle of hot water simmering on a spirit stove; the silver milk jug, sugar bowl, dish of freshly sliced lemon; cucumber sandwiches cut incredibly thin, hot muffins, and cake, both seed and plum; and she, poised with her cup of eggshell Minton ware, little finger crooked: "More tea, Georgie—Indian or China?"

Shaking his head in wonderment, he re-addressed himself for the fifth time to the ill-penned missive:

well eagle eye this joint where the said crown agents hang out is down by the river and the guy on the door wears a stove pipe hat like an old time preacher and i dont see him carrying no guns. all the time there are these other guys

going in and out and they are wearing black derby hats
and mostly with umbrellas only there aint been no rain
since we been in england which is crazy. the guy in the
stove pipe hat he wont let us in unless quote we state our
business end of quote. to do this would not be easy so we
stay outside and the next guy in a black derby who comes
out we grab and lean on somewhat. i ask him whats his
racket and he says hes the guy who buys up hay which he
ships out for indian elephants to eat in the dry season
when there aint no grass. on this subject he is very informative. in my opinion eagle eye these crown agent guys
are either crazy or on the level but whichever way theyre
harmless—tex

Well pleased with his aide's report which, with its brevity,
clarity of expression, ruthless excision of inessentials, and concise summing-up made it everything a report should be but
seldom is, George G. Sawtry cleared his mind of any lingering
doubts about the purchase. Through the good graces of the
eccentric but transparently honest Crown Agents, the Albert
Memorial would be his to give to that little girl over there with
the muffin in one hand and the teacup in the other, and her
little finger crooked as delicately as any queen's.

Throughout their brief association, Bunbury had never
questioned his accomplice about the latter's activities since
leaving the Irish Guards, nor had the other volunteered any
information on the subject save to mention, quite casually,
that he had been obliged to resign his commission for, as he
put it, "breaking the Eleventh Commandment, which says:
'Thou shalt not get found out committing any of the previous
ten.' " Why he had served prison sentences (and things he let
slip suggested that the recent sojourn in Brixton had not been
a unique experience) Bunbury could only conjecture. But it
did not call for much exercising of one's reason to figure out
that the errant Irishman had become, at some time in his
career, a confidence trickster—and a first-class one to boot.

Considering the Albert Memorial con: before ever he had devised the means to raise the two thousand "working money," O'Leary had already booked ahead the largest reception room in the prestigious Plantagenet Hotel—though he could have had, at that time, only the most sketchy outline in his mind as to how the con would be conducted. The spurious involvement of the Crown Agents, the splendid assurance of the authoritative letter of invitation, the neat manner by which the mark had been persuaded not to contact the senders (O'Leary himself was due to telephone George G. Sawtry that evening and secure his certain acceptance), all commanded Bunbury's admiration. About the raising of the working money—with the vision of Ms. Rosalind Purvis's gentle, trusting eyes as the pair of them lied their heads off to her—he felt less at ease, and only took comfort in his resolve to repay the money just as soon as the con was completed.

O'Leary broke in on his thoughts. They were sitting together in their room at the Gwynedd; while Bunbury had been thinking things over, his accomplice had been scribbling some notes by the window that looked out over the gardens of Paddington.

"Right, my dear Bunbury," said O'Leary, rising. "We've a couple of things to fix this afternoon, so we'd best divide forces —you to the Plantagenet to settle details for the auction and reception. I've made a list here of points to raise with the manager. Take a cab and have all the points off pat before you get to the hotel, there's a good chap. Now—the old Plantagenet is a fossilized relic of high Victoriana, and reminiscent of the days when our grandparents used to drape piano legs for decency's sake. That's why I chose it for the scene of the con. It absolutely exudes upper-middle-class respectability. I don't suppose any unmarried couple have spent a dirty weekend there since the place was built—and if anyone tried such a thing, the roof would probably fall in on them. From my observations, Americans of Sawtry's generation are as strait-laced as hell, the examples of such as Ulysses S. Grant and John Barrymore notwithstanding. Bear that in mind when settling details

with the manager, Bunbury old fellow, and you won't go far
wrong.

"And one last point: whatever happens, *we want no funny
business on the big night!*"

With this final, cryptic injunction, O'Leary dispatched his
junior partner in crime off on his errand, leaving himself to—
as he put it—"fix the rest of the distinguished guest list."

Like some faded Edwardian beauty turned dowager duchess, the Plantagenet Hotel graced Knightsbridge a stone's
throw from the Household Cavalry barracks, its comely red
brick mellowed by soot and time, the branches of the plane
tree in its forecourt supported by props and chains, and a
curious lassitude lying over all.

Bunbury paid off his cab and ascended the steps to the
revolving doors, which admitted him into a vast hallway smell-
ing of lavender floor polish, sandalwood, and pine. An announcement board on an easel was set up close by the door. In
stick-on lettering, he read an account of the day's doings in the
establishment:

Runnymede Room—Middlesex Clergy Annual Dinner
Crecy Rm—St Alice's Old Girls' Reunion
Agincourt Rm—Chess Tournament
Poitiers Rm—Old Fotheringhamians
Evesham Rm—Lecture: "Why Satan?"
Bosworth Rm—Mumbles

The activities at the Plantagenet appeared to put a pre-
mium on religion, old age, and indoor games in that order—
discounting Mumbles, whatever, or whoever, Mumbles might
be. It all squared with O'Leary's summing up of the place.

"Can I be of service, sir?" An elderly functionary in morning
tails came up behind him, soft-footed. He was as thin as a
crane, desiccated, sepulchral-voiced, but pink-cheeked as if he
had just ridden in a keen wind. "I am the manager. Ormerod is
my name."

"I've come concerning the booking of the Runnymede Room on the twenty-ninth," said Bunbury.

"Ah, you would be Colonel Abey, sir," said the other, this being the alias that O'Leary had adopted for the Plantagenet end of the operation.

"No, I am Dr. Judd," said Bunbury, in his persona for the occasion; and handed Ormerod a card that O'Leary had printed during lunchtime, the ink being barely dry. An unnecessary elegance on the face of it, the gesture went some way to establishing his *bona fides*.

D. G. R. Judd, M.A., Ph.D.
Deputy Chairman

Crown Agents for Oversea
Governments & Administrations

"Kindly walk this way, Dr. Judd," purred the manager, and he led Bunbury into a spacious office furnished with a partners' desk with a heavily tooled leather top and chairs of matching leather.

"Will you take tea, Doctor?"

"It is a little early for me, thank you," replied Bunbury, "and I'm due at Number Ten by four-thirty, so can we bring this matter to a point?"

"Please let us, sir." Ormerod was happy to accommodate anyone who was due to take tea with the Prime Minister. "What is your pleasure concerning the booking?"

"Firstly," said Bunbury, "there must be no publicity whatsoever, no matter how advantageous it may seem to the hotel."

The other threw up his hands in horror, and his gaunt cheeks turned even pinker with indignation, if that were possible.

"My dear sir, the very concept of . . . *publicity*"—he gave the word an edge of vileness, as if he were spitting it out—"is absolute anathema to the Plantagenet. We have not achieved the reputation we have, Dr. Judd, through grovelling to the gutter press!"

"Speaking for the Crown Agents, I'm glad to hear it," said Bunbury piously. Ormerod's statement squared with what O'Leary and he had surmised: the establishment had remained stuck in the latter half of the nineteenth century like a fly in amber, a posture that was slowly killing it. But it was an attitude that served their own requirements well.

"What more, sir?" asked Ormerod in a distant voice.

"The function will be in three parts," said Bunbury. "The first—an informal reception—will require the attendance of your staff to hand out drinks—a choice of champagne cocktails or dry sherry.

"The third and last part will call for some light entertainment of the decorous sort—I would hesitate to use the word 'cabaret,' which suggests something of a raffish nature. There will also be dancing till one-thirty. You can provide both a band and entertainment, I presume?"

Ormerod smiled. "Most happily," he said, "I have retained the services of Marcel and Félicité, who sing and dance in the modern manner. They are noted for their love duets from the shows of Coward, Novello, Rogers and Hammerstein, etc. They also dance quite divinely, having been runners-up in the European Ballroom Championships many times. As for music —we have our resident orchestra in Olivia Purbright and her Ladies, stalwarts of the Plantagenet for many years."

Bunbury exhaled a long, slow breath. "That sounds all very satisfactory, Mr. Ormerod," he said. "The orchestra, by the way, will be required to play the National Anthem at the commencement of the initial reception." He cocked a knowing eye in the other's direction.

Ormerod again turned a pinker shade of pink. "Doctor, you are not telling me that we are to expect . . . ?" His voice tailed away in awe.

"That is so," replied Bunbury. "Also present will be rulers of several emergent nations. I take it that—what was the name?

—Ms. Purbright and her Ladies will be able to play certain rather obscure national anthems from sight?"

"They are all . . . most accomplished," breathed Ormerod.

"Good. It only remains for me to touch upon the second, or central, part of the proceedings. . . ."

"Yes, Doctor?" The manager of the Plantagenet leaned forward so as not to miss a word.

"That part of the proceedings will last approximately a quarter of an hour, from eight-fifteen to eight-thirty. It will also be completely private, and all your staff will be excluded, without exception. It is to be . . . a secret investiture," lied Bunbury.

"A—*a secret investiture!*" whispered Ormerod.

And Bunbury knew that he had the manager of the Plantagenet "sewn up," as the saying goes. Or, to stretch the metaphor even further, "tied hand and foot and nailed to the ceiling."

Bunbury left the Plantagenet feeling rather chipper with himself for having carried out his commission commendably well, and telling himself that he had proved to be somewhat more than merely O'Leary's errand boy. Yes, distinctly, he had shown his mettle in the encounter with the manager—and the coming affair would run very smoothly.

One had grave misgivings about Marcel and Félicité—not to mention Olivia Purbright and her Ladies—but there was no doubt that O'Leary was correct in his summation that American males of George G. Sawtry's vintage were rather square, and harked back to the piping days of World War II—not unlike most Englishmen of the same boiling.

Being happily free of the burden of calling in at Number 10 Downing Street for tea, and mindful of the glorious summer weather, Bunbury decided to walk back to Sussex Gardens by way of Hyde Park.

In doing so, it might be said that he changed the course of his whole life—and the lives of several others.

"Major Arbuthnot—well, what a coincidence!"

Bunbury, strolling and wool-gathering in the sunshine, did not immediately react to his alias (one seldom does), but did a double-take when the girl in the pink-flowered dress turned to regard him. Even then he did not immediately recognize her. For one thing, she had the sun behind her; for another, she was without her glasses, and had done something or other quite bewitching with her formerly severe hair-do.

"Don't you remember me?" she asked.

"Why—Ms. Purvis!" he exclaimed. "Um—how nice."

"Did you get the cheque?" she asked.

"Yes, thanks so much. My acknowledgement's in the post."

"I never told you—but I liked your house very much."

"Thank you." Unaccountably—or accountably—he felt cheap.

"That's really what prompted me to put through the grant."

"You're very kind."

"Well . . ." She hesitated.

"Look—I wonder . . ."

"Yes?" Her eyes, he noticed for the first time, were of that elusive dark blue that's so nearly violet. And her hair was like ripe corn flowing free.

"Would you join me for tea?" he asked, gesturing to a café set just off the path: a place of dappled sunlight and shade, white napery, tinkle of cups and spoons. And there were empty tables. To his surprise, he found himself hanging breathless upon her reply.

"Why, that will be lovely. Actually, I was on my way there."

They found a table that was exactly half sunshine, half shadow. Rosalind Purvis ran her fingers through her hair and smiled across at him.

"You didn't recognize me, did you?" she challenged. "Don't deny it, I'm not offended. It's because I'm wearing my contact lenses."

"I never would have known," he said. "They—become you very well."

"Thank you. Tell me—do you miss the Army very much? You put in your letter of application that you're retired."

"I—I'm kept quite busy. I—um—buy and sell, you know."

"Were you ever married? You never touched on that in your letter."

"Nearly," he replied, "but not quite."

"Changed your mind at the last moment?"

"She changed it for me: I was left standing at the altar—just like in the song. She'd run off with my best friend."

She put her hand to her lips and stared at him, round-eyed.

"Oh, how awful of me to pry!" she said. "Whatever must you think?"

He paused, remembering that this was the first time he had ever confided the bald fact of his jilting to anyone. "Would it have made any difference to my application if you'd known?" he then asked. "I mean—being the sort of unstable chap that even a bride-to-be runs away from."

She shook her head vigorously. "Oh no," she replied. "We don't work like that. The quality of the house—architecturally and historically—is the first consideration. And then"—she looked squarely at him—"I always make a personal appraisal of the applicant. If I approve of him—his manners, the way he talks, whether he looks you straight in the eye, little things like nicely tended fingernails—then he's in." She laughed. "All very hit and miss, I'm afraid. I'm sure to pick a wrong 'un sooner or later—someone who'll just grab our money and bolt."

Bunbury was saved from having to make any comment on that by the arrival of the waitress to take their order. That done, he briskly changed the subject.

"And what about you?" he asked. "You style yourself in correspondence as 'Ms.' but that could mean anything nowadays."

"I'm divorced," she said. "And I'm 'Ms.' with my maiden name." I live with an old girl-friend I was at school with. Her name's Hannah McCracken and she's in public relations. As a matter of fact, she's supposed to be meeting me here for tea."

His covert glance took in the fact that she did not wear a wedding ring; his fair companion intercepted the glance, and smiled.

"I chucked it into the bottom of a ribbon box on the day my decree nisi came through," she explained cheerfully. "Not because I thought it any impediment to catching myself another man, but because I felt better without it."

Her outgoing frankness beckoned Horace Bunbury into hitherto unlit paths and uncharted holes and corners that had formerly been forbidden territory to him. He plunged in recklessly.

"I was absolutely desolate after Peri—after my fiancée left me standing," he said. "I'd never been a ladies' man and simply didn't know how to cope with it. A more worldly-wise chap, I suppose, would simply have thrown himself into a succession of shallow love affairs that were really quite fun. I had no such recourse . . ." he ended sadly.

"So what did you do?"

"I took to drink. I became—I suppose I became—an alcoholic."

"Oh dear!" The violet eyes were clouded with compassion. "How awful for you. And then what?"

"Luck intervened," he replied. "Quite by chance, I was given the opportunity to kick the habit. And I took it."

"Full marks to you!" she cried. "That *really* shows character. If there's anything I admire in a person it's the dogged-as-does-it approach to life, the picking up of one's circumstances and shaking them by the throat. Well done, Major Arbuthnot!" She was pink-cheeked with enthusiasm, and breathing heavily.

Any further extension of the pleasant intimacy that had sprung up between them unbidden was instantly dispersed by a shadow falling across their table, and a voice—a resonant and slightly nasal voice that carried well—greeting Bunbury's companion.

"Hi, Roz! Sorry I'm a bit late, but I got caught up at the last minute." Bunbury became the recipient of a long-lashed, dark-eyed glance of guarded appraisal. "Hello," she said, and he stood up.

"Hannah, this is Major Arbuthnot—Major, meet Hannah McCracken, whom I told you about." Rosalind Purvis seemed quite unaware of the sudden coolness of her friend's manner, and the concomitant restraint that had entered into his.

"Well, what have you been up to today, Roz?" The new-comer sat down, put on a pair of dark glasses, and addressed herself to her girl-friend, by her manner and introductory topic obliquely excluding their male companion.

Rosalind Purvis answered her, casting a glance and throwing a phrase from time to time in Bunbury's direction, to include him in the discourse; but the other woman refused to join in the game of politeness. By the time she had exhausted the subject of how both she and her friend had spent their day, whilst Bunbury had made a longueur of drinking a cup of tea and slowly chopping an Eccles cake into small pieces and masticating it with the speed of a caterpillar devouring a leaf, he was more or less no longer there.

It was then that the brunette turned her dark shades upon him, and "I see you wear a Guards tie, Major," she observed in her corncrake voice. "Which regiment?"

"The Coldstream. First Battalion," responded Bunbury, who had been briefed on the finer points by O'Leary.

"Retired?"

"Major Arbuthnot is now in the buying and selling business," interposed her friend, more forcefully than was absolutely necessary. She also seemed to be signalling a request for polite restraint to the emphatic Hannah—for which Bunbury was grateful.

"How interesting," was Hannah's comment. "And what, pray, do you buy and sell—Major?" she drawled.

"Statuary!" Bunbury blurted out the first word that sprang, unbidden, to his lips. He had not thought (nor had O'Leary) to arm himself with an occupation for his "retirement": the buying and selling notion had been merely a gut reaction.

"Oh, you're an art dealer!" cried Rosalind. "I had no idea.

You must know Dougal Winsor and Patrick Forster-Howe—
and most of the people at Christie's and Sotheby's, of course."

"Ah—some of them," replied Bunbury guardedly.

"Do you know Jack Howells and Peter Quill?" demanded
Hannah.

Some imp of intuition warned Bunbury to roll with the
punch.

"No, I don't," he said simply.

Rosalind frowned in mild puzzlement at her friend. "Who
are they, Han?" she asked.

"Oh, just old acquaintances," replied the other, looking
down into her teacup.

Bunbury made some brief business of glancing at his watch.

"I really must dash," he said. "It's been so nice seeing you
again, Ms. Purvis, and thank you for everything. 'Bye for now."

Rosalind Purvis gave him her hand and a warm goodbye;
Hannah McCracken did not offer her hand and responded
coolly to Bunbury's farewell—both of which her friend noted
with disfavour; as soon as their late companion was out of
earshot in the direction of the Serpentine bridge, she rounded
on the other.

"Han, you really are frightful when you try!" she said. "What
ever persuaded you to be so rude to that very nice and inoffen-
sive man? Go on—tell me!"

The other took off her shades and fixed her companion with
a level glance.

"He's shifty," she said. "Your Major Arbuthnot is shifty, and I
think he's a wrong 'un."

Rosalind Purvis pooh-poohed the idea. "Oh, come, my dear,
you hadn't met him for more than half a minute and you were
cold-shouldering him," she said. "The poor man wasn't being
shifty—just embarrassed at the way you deliberately cut him
out, and then started interrogating him like some dreadful
Gestapo agent."

"I don't need to study people deeply to size up their characters," responded Hannah, quite unrepentant. "I've been in

public relations all my working life and I'm knee-deep in phoneys all day long, so I can spot 'em a mile off.

"I repeat—your galloping major's a wrong 'un! And I'll tell you another thing: he went off and left you to pay for the tea."

Though Bunbury could have had no notion of just how badly he stood in Hannah McCracken's opinion, he was most uncomfortably aware of the appalling disparity between the relative atmospheres before and after the latter's arrival: with Rosalind, all sweetness and light; with the coming of Hannah, total disaster. The gloomy comparison occupied his mind all the way back to Sussex Gardens, so that he only vaguely sensed, rather than was pointedly aware of, the silver Rolls-Royce parked close by, but not immediately adjacent to, the Gwynedd Hotel; nor did he remark the five men who sat within it: two nondescript characters at the front; three much more noticeable types in the back—and one of them a giant in a curly-brimmed Homburg hat, from under which its owner glowered out at everyone, Bunbury included, who went in or out of the Gwynedd.

As for Hannah McCracken, she also was unable to get the tea-time encounter out of her mind, so much so that, at an early opportunity, she consulted her favourite almanac, from whose highly informative pages she obtained the address of the Foot Guards Record Office, which is Wellington Barracks, Birdcage Walk. A brief telephone conversation with a helpful quartermaster-sergeant there elicited that there was not, nor had there ever been, a Major Denys Arbuthnot, M.C., in any of the five regiments comprising the Guards' Division.

Unbeknownst to the two conspirators, their carefully contrived enterprise had sprung at least two potentially fatal leaks. . . .

FOUR

"I don't want to discuss the subject again, Hannah—it's closed!"

In their charming Georgian *cottage orné* in Kew, Rosalind Purvis and Hannah McCracken were having their fourth row in three days, and the fifth—or it might have been the sixth—since they shared their last toffee bar and swore lifelong loving friendship twenty-odd years previously.

"You're just burying your head in the sand, Roz!"

"All right—so I'm burying my head in the sand. I enjoy burying my head in the sand occasionally—it gives me a whole new perspective on life!"

"This guy is a phoney—and worse. And I have proof—"

"You've told me all that three times already!" blazed Rosalind. "So he claims to be somewhat grander than he is. All right, everyone's into that nowadays. It's called upward mobility and is highly commended. It's certainly no crime."

"He's impersonating an officer," said Hannah.

"That's no crime, either."

"I checked," said Hannah. "And it *is*."

"Oh." Rosalind looked away out of the window and blinked her eyes, discovering to her surprise that she was near to tears. And surely that was silly.

"Roz," said Hannah gently, "there's even more to it than that. Something else I've only just found out . . ."

"You've been digging around some more, have you?" snapped the other.

Hannah nodded. "You could call it that," she admitted. "Concerning this house of his that you so kindly donated four thousand quid to—"

"The house was genuine enough!" cried Rosalind. "I saw it with my own eyes! You can't take that away from him!"

"It isn't his for me to take off him," responded Hannah. She had a glossy weekly magazine in her hands. Opening it at one of the preliminary advertising pages, she laid it on the table before her friend. "Recognize it?"

Rosalind stared down at the page. It featured two large house ads put out by one of the prominent West End estate agents. The upper item and accompanying photo depicted a neat terraced house in Lochiel Street, Chelsea. It was the lower one of the pair that commanded her attention.

There was the house—*his* house. And she would have recognized it anywhere: the Edwardian period features enhancing the strong simplicity of the design, the touches of *fin de siècle* and restrained art nouveau. And the accompanying text: ". . . delightful gentleman's villa in secluded Wimbledon, yet within easy reach of the shops and the All-England Lawn Tennis Club. 4 bedrooms, 3 reception rooms and the usual offices . . . for sale by private treaty . . ."

"That proves nothing!" she cried, pushing the magazine aside. "So now he's put the house up for sale. Considering that we've given him a grant towards repairing the roof, it's reprehensible of him; but presumably he'll be in touch, to make some restitution . . ." She caught her friend's pitying glance and fell silent.

"Only—it isn't like that, is it, Han?" she said presently.

Hannah shook her head. "I checked with the agents," she said. "Digging around again, as you'd put it. The place has been on the market for months, but no takers—Edwardiana is not the flavour of the week. In fact they told me they'd had only one promising prospect, and that was a guy calling himself Major Arbuthnot, and he so impressed them that they took the unusual step of allowing him to have the key for an unchaperoned tour of the property.

"This was because he wanted—and I quote—to show his old mother round the house that they were hopefully going to make their home together, if she liked it.

"And that, Roz, was last Thursday—the day you went to see him there!

"Hi, Maw!" She grinned down at Rosalind.

It was not that Harriet was a callous or unfeeling person; it was simply that she could not resist investing even the most poignant circumstance with her own wry, gallows-style humour. It was all part of her elusive charm.

The great day dawned.

The two conspirators were up early. They were already going through the coming night's arrangements verbatim when they were interrupted by the arrival of Myfanwy with breakfast, which she served, as usual, in a shortie dressing-gown which she had the greatest difficulty in keeping together at the front. No sooner had she departed with one last lingering and longing glance in O'Leary's direction than they resumed work over eggs and bacon.

"The whole secret of this kind of operation," said O'Leary, "as in a set-piece battle which has been planned down to the last gaiter button, is to be prepared for the worst possible unexpected set-back and be ready to meet it with instant improvisation. Improvise—improvise—improvise—the secret of success. Don't forget that, feller, and be sure all will be well this night."

"I'll try to remember," said Bunbury.

They spent the whole morning going through the routine over and over again. After a light luncheon, both men climbed into their double bed and slept till the alarm bleeper woke them at four. They then rose, bathed, shaved, and dressed in tuxedos (Bunbury had hired his).

The plan called for an early arrival at the Plantagenet half an hour before the scheduled appearance of the guests, to make sure that everything was in order to receive them, and also to have the ladies' orchestra run through the national and two other state anthems—the latter pair had been lovingly arranged by a hack contrapuntalist of Denmark Street, Soho. O'Leary, as befitted his seniority in the partnership, was to station himself in the hallway to receive the distinguished guests—particularly George G. Sawtry and his lady.

(Oddly, the Irishman averred that he already knew the American quite well. On the occasion that he had telephoned the mark to receive his heartfelt acceptance of the invitation, Sawtry had gleefully informed him that the Albert Memorial was going to be his little lady's wedding present, yes sir! And it didn't matter if he had to bid right to his limit for this piece of real estate—hers it was going to be!)

As the critical hour of their departure drew near, Bunbury was pleased to notice his accomplice's splendid high spirits. Myfanwy, who had served them luncheon in their room that day (for security reasons they never ate with their fellow guests), flirted with O'Leary as usual, and received a lively response from him—to her manifest delight.

At six forty-five precisely, a knock on their room door announced Myfanwy with the news that the minicab they had ordered was at the door. Each made a last check of his bow-tie in the mirror, and they went downstairs, where the hall telephone was ringing.

Myfanwy answered it. "Hello, the Gwynedd Hotel at your service, we always strive to please. What—will you repeat that, please? . . .

"It's for you, Mr. O'Leary!"

"Who is it, Myfanwy?"

"He didn't say, Mr. O'Leary—only that it's important."

O'Leary shrugged at Bunbury and took the phone, announcing himself. Moments later he looked back, his hand over the mouthpiece.

"You go on, Bunbury," he said. "This may take a little while, but I'll be right behind you."

"Okay," said the latter. "But don't cut it too fine."

The first item on the announcement board read:

Runnymede Room—Private Reception

Mr. Ormerod was waiting for him. The manager was in white tie and tails and scented like the Garden of Eden.

"All's ready, Dr. Judd," he purred, "and this"—indicating a large man by his side—"is our resident emcee, Mr. Fotheringhay, who will have the honour of announcing your guests."

"Pleased to meet you, Doctor." Fotheringhay was big enough to double for the hotel bouncer, with a grip like a gorilla and a chest that threatened to burst his dress-shirt studs wide open.

"Come and see the room, sir," fussed Ormerod. "I think you'll agree that the Plantagenet has done you proud."

The Runnymede was the size of a modest ballroom, with a flower-bedecked stage at one end, upon which were grouped four females of indeterminate years; clad in long frocks and seated in proximity to their instruments—piano, violin, clarinet, double-bass—they were clearly Olivia Purbright and her Ladies' Orchestra.

A quick check around the room assured Bunbury that the hotel had indeed done them proud: the place contained enough floral arrangements to restock Kew Gardens, and must be costing the earth. The drinks table, attended by fully a dozen waiters, was also lavishly provided with sufficient champagne to launch a battle fleet.

"I think," he said, "that I should like to hear the national and other anthems."

"Forward, Miss Purbright!" cried Ormerod.

The orchestra leader, who also made some shift at playing the piano while conducting, introduced Bunbury to her consoeurs, who then rendered one complete verse of "God Save the Queen" right through with riffs and no mistakes. They were slightly less certain of touch with the two state anthems of emergent nations, particularly with the second one—but since this had been transcribed from the original orchestration of nose-flute and bongo drums, it was perhaps not to be wondered at.

And where, said Bunbury to himself, when the last strains died away, is O'Leary, damn him? . . .

It's already ten past seven, and the early birds—the thirsty buggers—will be arriving any minute now!

"Admiral Sir William and Lady Windrush!"

Representing the vanguard of the thirsty brigade, this epitome of the sea-dog breed wore three rows of medals, the sash and star of the Bath, an interesting-looking cross dangling under his white tie, and an incredibly thin and rangy wife trailing in his wake. Bunbury introduced himself and directed the pair towards the drinks table, to which they moved with immoderate haste.

(But where was O'Leary? Supposing Sawtry arrived first, and he, Bunbury, had to greet him? Of course, a lot of water had passed under a lot of bridges since his first encounter with the Texan, but though no longer bearded, emaciated, ragged, and drink-sodden, might not Sawtry recognize him still? In their most careful planning, they had never reckoned to submit him to the mark's close inspection.)

"The Lord Bunting of Cheame," declaimed emcee Fotheringhay. "His Honour Judge Copplestone and Mrs. Copplestone . . ."

They were coming thick and fast: he could see a mass of faces crowding in through the revolving doors and into the hallway. With a fixed grin on his face and one eye constantly roving for the sight of his accomplice, Bunbury greeted them all and introduced himself.

"His Grace the Duke of Cumberland . . ."

"Captain and Mrs. Weir . . ."

"Mr. and Mrs. George G. Sawtry."

Bunbury stiffened—as towards him strode the diminutive figure of the Texan in black silk tuxedo and string tie, still wearing his white Stetson. Upon his arm was quite the most ravishing-looking brunette Bunbury had ever set eyes on outside the silver screen.

It was the moment of truth. He extended his hand to the mark.

"Good evening, sir," he purred as best he was able. "My

name is Judd—Crown Agent, you know—and your co-host for tonight."

Sawtry, stridently emitting the leathery reek of his favourite Old Chaps cologne, shook hands vigorously, his keen eyes searching Bunbury's face and weighing him up; to his intense relief, the latter saw no sign of recognition there; merely the appraisal of a man used to taking stock of his fellow men and filing them away in some compartment of his mind.

"Nice to meet you, sir," said the Texan, and he introduced "Judd" to the ravishing creature by his side.

"Champagne cocktail, Mrs. Sawtry?" murmured Bunbury, as a waiter hovered near and the lady's spouse was already helping himself.

"Do you have Vichy water?" she responded loudly.

"That's my little girl," declared Sawtry, his eyes soft with fondness. "Liquor never passes her dainty lips. No sir! A model of rectitude and an example to all women. That's my Desirée!"

Bunbury opined that it was very charming, and Vichy water was brought for the lady.

"Where is Colonel Abey?" asked the mark, mentioning the cover name for O'Leary in the present phase of the con. "The colonel and I, though we have only conversed on the telephone, already have a considerable rapport"—the little Texan looked to left and right, as if to ensure that they were not overheard by anyone in the chattering throng surrounding them—"and I made it abundantly clear to him that I am backing down for no man in this coming auction, for I bet my ceiling price is one helluva lot higher than any three guys in this room would form syndicate and raise against me." He nudged Bunbury in the ribs. "Heh! And I also bet you'd give your eye-teeth to know my ceiling price, Mr. Crown Agent—right?"

Five million dollars, said Bunbury—but not out loud.

"Right!" He grinned sheepishly, then added, "My colleague Colonel Abey will be a little late. He's been held up at the—ah —palace. But he'll be along shortly."

(God, let it be so! Or how am I going to handle this shemozzle, the auction and all?)

The Texan's attention sharpened. "Speaking of the palace," he said. "When are you expecting"—he lowered his voice— *"you know who?"*

"Imminently," replied Bunbury. "Don't worry, she'll be on time. As the saying goes: punctuality is the politeness of—er— Royalty.

"Excuse me a moment, Mr. Sawtry," he added, discerning a signal from over by the drinks table, "the Duke of Cumberland wants a word with me."

Relieved to be free of the mark's probings, Bunbury approached the tall and distinguished figure whose arrival had caused a considerable stir among the staff of the Plantagenet a little while earlier. He was scooping peanuts into his mouth and swilling them down with deep draughts of champagne. He frowned testily at Bunbury, whom he had never met but only heard of.

"Where the hell's O'Leary?" he demanded.

"I don't know," confessed Bunbury. There seemed no point in dissembling to this character. "He was supposed to be right behind me, but that was an hour ago."

The other pulled a long lip. "Well, I hope you guys know your business," he said, "but I did warn O'Leary when I set this trick up for him that he'd better be here, and the money with him—in cash!" He took another fistful of peanuts, another swig of vintage champagne enlivened by vintage cognac of a notable provenance. "The boys and girls won't like it if they don't get paid on the dot, and they're quite capable of turning nasty and breaking up the joint. This isn't the *cream* of the acting profession we're dealing with, feller. These are a load of personable bums who've been resting too long and been deprived of their booze. Of whom Freddie and Liza, there, are pretty good examples," he added, gesturing towards the seadog and his consort—the first to arrive, and now remaining upright only by the support of the drinks table.

Bunbury's reply was cut short by the approach of George G.

Sawtry and his bride. The former sidled up to him and murmured in his ear, "Did you say 'Duke'—that guy's a *duke?*"

Bunbury nodded.

"No kidding?"

"No kidding," Bunbury assured him. And with a clear conscience—for Gerald Glenvile Arthur de la Tour Jobling, confirmed bachelor, unemployed actor, and part-time con man, was incidentally a real live duke, and of all that fraudulent gathering the only genuine item.

Gerald Jobling, 12th Duke of Cumberland and Wye, it was who chaperoned they whom he privately referred to as "the mark and his missus" through the next part of the proceedings; for this was his brief—in addition to assembling the motley crew of failed and aspiring Thespians who comprised the "distinguished guests." To this end, he introduced Mr. and Mrs. Sawtry to the more attractive and articulate of the gathering, carefully avoiding those—and they were many—who had already made great inroads into the free drink. Freed of the burden of the Sawtrys, Bunbury was able to devote his whole attention to worrying about the non-arrival of his senior partner in crime, to which end he made continuous sorties out into Knightsbridge, peering to left and right along the busy street, watchful for a taxi in all that bustling evening throng that might be carrying Thomas O'Leary.

He had no such luck. . . .

Upon his third attempt, he got no further than the hallway before a black Daimler limousine drew up outside the revolving doors and a legion of flunkeys mobbed around, opening passenger doors, handing out a striking-looking woman in a blazing tiara, along with two couples in resplendent flowing robes and turbans, girt about with barbaric jewellery that was rivalled by flashing eyes, gleaming teeth.

The guests of honour had arrived!

Bunbury just had time to dart back into the Runnymede Room, alert the emcee, flag Gerald Jobling, and point a commanding finger at Olivia Purbright and her Ladies before *they* were being bowed into the reception room by the manager and his acolytes.

And then, upon Olivia Purbright's descending beat, the orchestra struck up the national anthem.

"The Princess is looking very fine tonight," said Gerald Jobling aside to his companion.

"But I thought," said Sawtry, with a note of disappointment, "that we were to expect . . ."

"Prior engagement, old chap," said the duke. "Her Royal Highness—a third cousin, y'know—is frightfully amusing. Also a patron of the arts. The two of you will get along splendidly."

"Is that so?" said the mark, fingering his bow-tie. "You really think so, Duke?"

At the close of all three anthems—in the last of which the violiniste was emboldened to interpolate a protracted cadenza, quite extempore, into that part of the melody normally carried by the nose-flute—Bunbury went forward to do the honours that had originally been scripted for O'Leary.

He bowed deeply from the waist to the regal figure in the tiara.

"Your Royal Highness," he said. "This is indeed an honour. . . ."

And to the rulers of the two emergent nations: "Your Excellencies, this is indeed an honour. . . ."

Also sticking to the script, the duke brought forward Mr. and Mrs. George G. Sawtry, to present them to the principal guest of honour; but before effecting the introduction and leaving them together, he contrived to take the splendid-looking lady to one side, and a surprisingly homely conversation ensued.

"How's it going, darling?" she whispered.

"Not well at all, m'love," responded the duke. "O'Leary hasn't turned up with the tin, and some of the cast are practically screw-eyed with bubbly. I think it would be a good idea to bail out immediately after the phoney auction."

"Fine by me," she said. "What shall we do—have dinner out, or go back to the flat?"

"Anything in the fridge?"

"Half a salmon. Plenty of salad. Bottle of Chablis chilled."

"Lead me to it," said the duke. "See you later, darling." Gesturing the Sawtrys forward, he added, "Your Royal Highness, I have the greatest pleasure to present, all the way from Texas . . ."

As the hands of the clock crept around to a quarter past eight, Bunbury allowed himself the slender commendation of having conducted the first part of the proceedings more or less disaster-free. Taking all in all, he supposed that the worst was over, and even if O'Leary did not turn up at all (and what *had* happened to him?), the second and third parts of the proceedings would be more or less all downhill. He had attended many auctions, at the great London art dealers' and elsewhere, and the role of auctioneer had never struck him as anything that a man of average intelligence, education, presence of mind, and firmness of spirit could not tackle on his head. (He took another deep quaff of the same temperance beverage that was favoured by the dishy Mrs. Sawtry, and thanked his lucky stars that his judgement was no longer clouded by alcohol.)

As for part three, the entertainment and dancing: with the auction over, the memorial safely "sold" to Sawtry, and the mark's cheque tucked in his pocket, no further problems remained. He could actually relax and enjoy himself. Dance and be merry. He might even—and the thought curiously excited him—have a decorous turn around the floor with the dishy Mrs. Sawtry. . . .

A voice at his elbow—a slightly slurred voice—aroused him from his wool-gathering. It was the mark himself, and by his speech and his unsteady gait, the Texan multimillionaire had obviously imbibed deeply of the grape.

"I shuppose that you're just about ready to begin the auction, huh?" asked Sawtry, taking a pull at an enormous cigar and smiling benignly at his addressee.

"Any moment now, sir," replied Bunbury. "Enjoying the reception?"

"Be-yootiful—be-yootiful!" intoned Mr. Sawtry.

"Having a good time, then?"

"Never so much in all my life," declared the mark. "When I tell you . . ." He laid a hand on Bunbury's arm. "When I tell you . . ."

"Yes?"

"The Princess—lovely lady—lovely! She shed to me—y'know wha' she shed to me?"

"No, sir, I don't."

"Her Royal Highness, she shed to me—she promised that she'd come over to Texas and dedicate the memorial when it's been re-erected. Now—wha' d'you thing of that, huh?"

"Wonderful news, sir," said Bunbury. "It's to be hoped that your bid is successful."

With the unexpected cunning of the near-inebriated, Sawtry tapped the side of his nose and said, "My bid will win okay, Mister Smarty-Pants Crown Agent. Only—I don't aim to go one cent above my ceiling price.

"Get it?"

It was behind schedule—past eight-thirty—before the room was cleared of hotel employees and the distinguished guests and putative bidders were gathered before the drinks table, now denuded of all but a sheet of paper and a gold propelling pencil which Bunbury, in his persona of auctioneer, had produced from his breast pocket and laid before him.

"Your Royal Highness, Your Excellencies, my lords, ladies, and gentlemen . . ."

A silence fell upon the gathering as Bunbury declaimed. Then someone sniggered, but was immediately shushed to shamefaced silence.

"The item of real estate offered for sale is the edifice known as the Albert Memorial," said Bunbury, reading from notes. "The item is offered free of all encumbrances but without a site. Details of the conditions of sale are contained within the schedule which all of you will have received within the last few days. I will run over the salient points which apply particularly to this specific sale.

"All bids are to be made in United States dollars.

"At the conclusion of the sale, the successful bidder will render immediate payment by cheque, made out to cash. This, I would point out, is to facilitate the special arrangements which the Crown Agents have made with the Bank of England.

"Lastly, by order of the Department of the Environment, the dismantling and transportation of the said monument will be the responsibility of the Crown Agents, who will deliver the said monument to any designated site in the United Kingdom, or in the case of an overseas sale, to the London docks or Heathrow Airport—dependant upon the purchaser's choice. And the cost of dismantling and transportation, together with insurance, will be borne by the Crown Agents. And upon the discharge of this requirement, the responsibility of the said Crown Agents will cease."

At the end of his peroration, Bunbury drew a deep breath and picked up his gold propelling pencil.

"The sale will now commence. Who will open the bidding? What am I offered?

"A hundred thousand dollars?"

Someone nodded—it was the Duke of Cumberland.

"A hundred thousand to His Grace," intoned Bunbury.

A hand was raised.

"Two hundred thousand."

Another.

"Three hundred."

A nod from the front.

"Four hundred. We will proceed in steps of two hundred thousand," declared Bunbury, who was in his element. It was like—*it was like being God!* "And the bidding is against you, Your Grace," he added.

A nod from the duke.

"Six hundred thousand dollars is bid—thank you, Your Grace." It was in Cumberland's script to bring up the bidding to around three million, then drop out for a while, let the mark coast along with a couple of the more reliable characters, and then move in again to bid Sawtry up to his five-million limit.

But—*where the hell was Sawtry?*

A new hand went up.

"Eight hundred thousand—Captain Weir." During the reception Bunbury had busied himself in memorizing the faces in the script.

"ONE AND A HALF MILLION DOLLARS!"

There was no mistaking those cadences—they rolled like the boundless great plains of George G. Sawtry's native Texas!

"A million and a half is bid," declared Bunbury. "We will now proceed in steps of half a million!"

Sawtry had moved up near the front so that he was in full view of the auctioneer. The duke was at the rear of the crowd, but his great height marked him out like a crane among ducks: he nodded to Bunbury.

"Two million dollars is bid. It's against you, Mr. Sawtry," said Bunbury.

"TWO AN' A HALF!"

"Three million dollars."

And so it went on. The duke dropped out, as arranged. With tantalizing hesitancy, Weir and another scripted bidder brought the pot from three to four—Sawtry abstaining.

And then—an entirely new voice; a voice, moreover, that was so slurred as to be almost incoherent.

"Ah bid the sum of four an' a half—hic!—million dollarsh!"

The bid came from right under Bunbury's nose. The *soi-disant* Admiral Sir William Windrush lifted his head, gazed up at the auctioneer with glazed eyes and a fatuous grin, and hiccuped again. His rangy lady wife, who was asleep standing up with her head on his shoulder, gave a throaty giggle and went back to sleep again.

Bunbury threw Sawtry a frantic glance and raised his gold propelling pencil, questioningly.

"Five million!" snapped the multimillionaire with an air of finality, and Bunbury made as if to bring down his pencil.

"Wait!—wasser marra with my bids, hey? My monish ash

good ash ish ish!" The self-styled admiral was not only boozed and showing off, but truculent with it.

Sawtry was shaking his head. Desirée was in tears. Bunbury was staring in awful fascination at Windrush, who opened his mouth to wreck the entire con—hook, line, and sinker.

In an awesome silence, the "admiral" grinned inanely, hiccuped—and fell flat on his face. His lady wife, bereft of support, folded up with an infinite grace and fell elegantly on top of him.

Bunbury brought the end of his pencil down upon the table-top. It made a resounding tap.

"Sold to Mr. George G. Sawtry for five million dollars!" he breathed.

The process by which the remainder of that evening developed from the sort of thing that was tailor-made for Royalty, not to mention such models of stern and unbending respectability as Mr. and Mrs. George G. Sawtry, was never quite clear to Horace Bunbury; the reason for the affair's further slide into an orgy of total abandonment evaded him entirely.

A beginning may have been made with the retirement of the mark himself when, having been relieved of his five-million-dollar cheque, Sawtry displayed a tendency to nod off to sleep, and his ever-considerate bride prevailed upon the management to provide him with an armchair in a quiet room— after which she repaired to the buffet table that had been furnished in the Runnymede Room and ate her way through a heaped plateful of York ham, smoked salmon, game pie, coleslaw, and potato salad, followed by strawberry and loganberry cheesecake with Devonshire clotted cream. She also essayed to try—for the first time ever, so she assured the credulous Bunbury—a sip or two of champagne. By the time he left her after a few minutes' desultory conversation between her mouthfuls, Mrs. Sawtry had corralled a two-litre bottle of Krug for herself and was already well down it.

Despite the efforts of Olivia Purbright and her Ladies, who devotedly went through their repertoire of the golden oldies immortalized through strict-tempo ballroom dancing popularized in the 1950s, not a soul was to be prised free of the buffet and drinks. The advent of Marcel and Félicité and their renditions of love duets brought only catcalls, and the markedly mannered style of their dancing called forth the most derisory imitations from the few—the very few—who staggered out onto the floor.

It was the gorgeous Mrs. Sawtry who dictated the ultimate tone of the proceedings by leaping lithely onto the drinks table (and she by this time with the better part of two litres of champagne tucked beneath her skimpy belt) to give an exhibition of go-go dancing which drove her onlookers wild, particularly when, in the furtherance of an unmistakably professional knowledge of the Terpsichorean art quite obviously derived through years of assiduous practice, she felt constrained to divest herself of all her upper garments and a fair amount of the nether.

The change of tempo—musical and moralistic—then persuaded Ms. Olivia Purbright to let rip in a riotous exhibition of boogie-woogie piano playing that she had picked up during the hard times of her student days at the Royal College, when she had kept body and soul intact by playing gigs in sleazy Soho clubs. Her ladies joined in with commendable abandon.

The "Princess" took no part in this rout, but signalled with her eyes for the duke to take her home, which he did. No such inhibition troubled the four exotic characters playing the roles of excellencies and ladies; catching the mood of the moment, they built uprights and a crossbar and, after removing all or most of their resplendent flowing robes, proceeded to exhibit the kind of limbo dancing that is seldom seen outside its native habitat.

Pretty soon the entire company—or those who could stand up—were limbo-dancing in an extended conga line right round the vast room and under the crossbar, which was put lower and lower as the frenzy developed.

By eleven o'clock the entire gathering was into boogie-woogie, go-go, or limbo, and the dance floor was littered with discarded apparel. Dominating it all was the near-nude Mrs. George G. Sawtry, who had been picked up by emcee Fotheringhay in a flashy adagio, and whose lithe, expensively tanned form was being tossed between him and two brawny Plantagenet waiters—while her spouse slept peacefully in the next room.

It was at this stage that Horace Bunbury, quite appalled, slunk away unnoticed. His last glimpse of the orgy was a vignette of the double-bass player—a lady of fairly advanced years and considerable *embonpoint*—taking five bars' rest to extract from the inner recesses of her instrument case a quart bottle of Guinness's stout and putting it to her lips.

He went back to Sussex Gardens by taxi, glad to have escaped from the rout, and thankful that the participants were all too far gone to have remembered their fees.

Yes, notwithstanding everything—forgetful of the shambles he had left back there, disregarding the hideous moment when one more breath from that drunken fool Windrush would have destroyed the whole thing entirely—despite all that, he had won through completely off his own bat. And he had the mark's cheque to prove it.

He took the cheque from his wallet and read it over and over again—so delightful did the words and music of five million smackers sound in the ear—till he reached the Gwynedd Hotel.

He had a front door key and let himself in quietly. He tiptoed up the stairs, wondering all the time if O'Leary would be waiting up for him, no doubt to apologize with a very sound explanation for leaving him in the lurch (and, by golly, after what he had achieved on his own, there would be an end to this junior partner lark!).

Somewhat to his surprise, the bedroom door was locked, but it opened readily to his own key. As a further surprise, the light switch brought no illumination, and when he had groped his way over to try his bedside lamp, he found that there was no longer a bulb in the socket. Edging round the big double bed, he went over to the window and dragged back the curtains. And there, by the thin illumination of a half moon, he saw his partner's tousled head on his pillow.

"O'Leary!" he exclaimed. "Wake up! I've got the cheque— we're millionaires, old man!"

No reply. The fellow had simply locked himself in, gone to bed, and gone to sleep.

Drunk, no doubt—too drunk to even give a damn about the five million! After having left me holding the baby, he hadn't even the courtesy to stay awake and sober, to hear the marvellous news.

Too tired and fed up to grope his way to the wash-basin and scrub his teeth, let alone attend to any more protracted ablutions, Bunbury simply kicked off his shoes, shrugged out of jacket and shirt, dropped his trousers, and fell into bed as he was. His thought was to growl good night to his companion; but it seemed on reflection to be an entirely undeserved civility.

He turned over to go to sleep with his back to the other— and inadvertently hacked his bedmate in the shin.

"Sorry," he growled.

No reply.

"And bugger you, too," muttered Bunbury.

O'Leary was certainly sleeping soundly. Not a murmur out of him. Can't even hear him breathing. . . .

Motivated by nothing more than common curiosity, he gave another fairly hefty shove against the other's leg. It brought no response whatsoever: not a stir, not even a mutter of complaint.

Bunbury sat up in bed. "Are you all right, old chap?" he demanded, taking his companion's shoulder, and finding it curiously—stiff. . . .

"Oh, my God—O'Leary!"

He shook the other vigorously. The tousled head lolled sideways towards him. Even in the thin moonlight, he could see the gaping mouth and the opened eyes that stared sightlessly up into his.

And then Horace Bunbury began to scream!

FIVE

His cries roused the house. By the time he had leapt out of the bed of sudden horror, they were pounding on the door.

"What is it—what's going on in there?" someone shouted.

He had reached the door and was wrenching at the handle when it flew open in his face. A tall figure, silhouetted against the light in the landing, turned to address a crowd of frightened people.

"It's all right, folks. My friend has these attacks from time to time. No harm done. Go back to bed, Myfanwy dear."

The door was shut again. And the two of them were inside.

"Phew!" exhaled O'Leary. "Thank God you're back."

"It—it's—*you!*" whispered Bunbury, striving hard to hang on to the rags of his sanity. "But why—where? I thought you . . ." He pointed to the shadowy bed and the thing upon it.

"What did I do with those damned light bulbs?" growled O'Leary, rummaging. "Ah—here we are."

Reaching, he plugged a bulb into the overhead socket and the room was instantly flooded with light. He cursed and wrenched the thing out again. "For Pete's sake draw those bloody curtains!" he hissed. "Do you want to get us both twenty years' hard labour?"

Bunbury hastened to obey. The light came on again. Slowly, by easy stages, because it hurt, he let his gaze pan towards the thing in the bed, as it lay there, half uncovered, wearing a black shirt and black trousers. His horrified gaze was directed to the face: it was a harsh, angry face, staring-eyed, the mouth open as if to shout fury; black-jowled, black-haired.

"Who—who's—*he?*" whispered Bunbury.

"Name of Darkie Todd," was the response. "The underworld gave him the nickname, his old mother no doubt picked out the surname with a pin. Give me a hand to fix him up and get him out of here."

"Where to?" asked Bunbury.

"Anywhere. As far as possible," retorted the other. "Or how are we going to laugh him off when Myfanwy comes in here to make the bed? Come on, man—don't let me have to do *everything!*"

Reluctantly, shrinking, Bunbury took hold of the dead man's ankles and helped lift him out of the bed. The corpse was dressed from head to foot in black: shoes, socks, and all. They laid him on the floor. Bunbury, whose acquaintance with death was severely limited, was hard put to summon up an attitude of mind for coping.

"The jacket's over there where I threw it," said O'Leary. "We'll fix him up with a tie. A mackintosh, too, I think. And a hat will come in useful to hide the face." He went over, opened his cabin trunk, and came out with the requisite items.

"Look—I say," began Bunbury. "Can't you tell me what this is all about? I mean . . ." He spread his hands to encompass the corpse, the hotel bedroom; implying the rooms above, below, all round them—full of *people* who would also want to know. . . .

"I'll explain along the way," said O'Leary. "We've only ten minutes or so—less—to catch the last train."

"The last train—to *where?*" cried Bunbury, aware that his voice held a note of hysteria that was cracking in the upper register.

"Bristol, I expect," responded O'Leary vaguely. "Give me a hand with this mackintosh. Hold him upright. That's the ticket.

"Now we'll both slip a few clothes on and be off." He was in a dressing-gown with nothing under.

Another question nagged at Bunbury. "Where were you when I arrived back?" he demanded.

O'Leary, struggling hastily into his trousers, replied, "I locked the door but took the bulbs out in case Jones-Evans or his missus came blundering in with a key. Then I went and climbed into bed with Myfanwy." He scowled to see Bunbury staring at him in high indignation. "Jesus, Mary, and Joseph— would you have me sitting here with a bloody corpse till you deigned to come home?

"Hey—speaking of life and death, did you get the cheque?"

"I thought you'd never ask. Yes, I did."

"Good man!"

By then they had Darkie Todd dressed and standing upright, a trilby hat cocked rakishly over one eye and shielding the whole of the upper part of the face. Gingerly Bunbury looped the dead right arm over his left shoulder—as his accomplice had done the other side.

"Right!" said O'Leary. "To Paddington Station—fast!"

No one heard them go downstairs—at least, no one responded to their tread or stirred when they let themselves out of the front door and into the short street—no more than two or three hundred yards—that led directly to Paddington mainline station and the looming bulk of the Great Western Royal Hotel.

They set off down the road, and Darkie Todd trailed his dead feet as best as he was able; they looked for all the world like a couple of half-drunks helping a dead-drunk friend home.

"I only hope," said O'Leary, "that we don't run into some smart young copper on the make."

No such apparition barred their progress. Unhindered, they came to the ramp leading down to the station concourse. Isambard Kingdom Brunel's great train hall was silent save for a solitary voice raised in song: it echoed as in a cathedral. Leaving Bunbury and the corpse slumped together on a bench, O'Leary went to fetch tickets and was soon back.

"The last train's out in three minutes," he said. "Let's go."

A sleepy black collector punched their tickets: single to Bristol and two platform ticketeers to see him off. "You've only got two minutes," he warned them.

Almost the first carriage they came to was ideal: empty save for a rangy figure seated there alone. There was a half-full bottle of scotch on the table before him; he looked round with a glad smile to see company, but his eyes were glazed and unfocussed.

"Greetings, gentlefolk!" he hailed them. "Are you for Bristol?"

"Our friend is," said O'Leary. "Will you look after him? He's half-asleep and a bit boozed."

"Rest easy, friend," said the cheerful drunk. "We are all equals on the midnight fornicator. I will entertain your comrade with talk of the town. What are his interests?"

"Anything you say will interest him," responded O'Leary, tipping the corner of the single ticket to Bristol in the corpse's hatband so that the guard could punch it when he came round. "But don't expect much in the way of repartee. Good night to you."

"Good night, my friends." The cheerful drunk waved to them as they stood outside and watched the train slide slowly away and gather speed. The last they saw was Darkie Todd's new friend bend to address a remark to his bowed, shielded head.

Not a word passed between them till they were clear of the station. As the end of the road and the Gwynedd came in sight, Bunbury said, "I suppose no one will rumble that he's dead till they reach Bristol and clear the train."

"They might even let him sleep it off—as they suppose— when the train's shunted into a siding for the night," said O'Leary. "In any event, there's nothing to connect him with us now—nothing."

Bunbury glared at his companion with some heat. "There's the chap who clipped the tickets at the barrier!" he snapped. "Not to mention the drunk on the train!"

O'Leary shrugged that off. "The guy at the barrier never even looked our way," he said. "As for the drunk—he'll have forgotten us by now."

There being no response to such airy assurance, Bunbury let the issue pass; nor did his companion seem to wish to pursue it.

"Tell me how everything went off tonight," he said. "Any snags crop up?"

"Plenty," replied Bunbury, adding tartly, "Starting with your non-appearance, just about everything that could have gone wrong did. We nearly lost the bidding to one of the no doubt stony-broke Thespians you had the duke organize. The girl who played the Princess was very good. Everyone else, Mrs. Sawtry included, got stoned and outrageous. But—yes—Sawtry handed over his cheque." They reached the hotel and O'Leary made to put his key in the lock, but Bunbury forestalled him by laying a hand on his arm. "Look, let's get one thing settled, O'Leary," he said. "Had that guy Darkie's death anything to do with the phone call you got tonight?"

"Yes."

"Then what was it all about?"

"Nothing to do with our present enterprise," replied O'Leary. "That I promise you. It was . . . just a little unfinished business from my past, and it doesn't concern you at all."

"It concerns me very much!" snapped Bunbury. "I've already made myself an accessory after the fact by helping you to conceal a murder.

"You did murder him, I suppose?"

"Matter of fact, I didn't," said O'Leary.

They went on up and to bed without exchanging another word till the light was out.

"What next?" asked Bunbury. "About the con, I mean?"

"Council of war tomorrow after breakfast," replied O'Leary. "Till then, go to sleep and dream about how that two and a half million's going to sweeten your existence.

"See you in dreamland—I shall be the guy in the yacht, with a blonde on one knee and a brunette on the other.

"Night, Bunbury."

"Good night, O'Leary," replied the other stiffly.

The fine, sunny weather continued and had that morning been officially designated a heat wave. They checked out of the Gwynedd and deposited their luggage at the station, then went for breakfast to one of those delightful small cafés in Paddington that put tables and potted trees outside the pavement during summery weather, Paris fashion.

They both ordered coffee and croissants. Bunbury had bought a copy of the *Courier* and was avidly scanning the Home News page in the expectation of reading how the police had been summoned to the Plantagenet Hotel in the early hours by irate guests complaining about the reincarnation of Sodom and Gomorrah that was being re-enacted in the Runnymede Room. No such report appeared; the Home News was largely concerned with a lightning shipping strike that threatened to disrupt the Channel ports, but was not expected to spread.

"You've brought the cheque?" demanded O'Leary.

"Would I leave it behind?" retorted his companion.

"Right—to work, to work!"

They had already sketched out the next stage of the operation, and O'Leary went through it again in detail.

"Two things to do, both in quick time," he said. "First, to process that cheque, so that, by tonight or earlier, it really represents five million lovely dollar bills, instead of a piece of paper whose only function—given certain circumstances—would be to finger us. This process is known in the profession as laundering.

"Second, we've got to make ourselves scarce before the mark cottons on to the fact that the Crown Agents are not going to deliver the merchandise, not this week, next week, or ever. To that end, we are going abroad—as far abroad as possible. And as soon as possible, before Sawtry blows the whistle on us and all the airports are alerted for us. For my money, that means we move out today. Agreed?"

"Agreed," said Bunbury. "Now, how do we go about processing the cheque—laundering it, I mean."

"I have this friend," said O'Leary, "who runs a cosy little merchant bank in the City. Pillar of the Church, father of six, big shot in the Masons, Freeman of the City of London, city counsellor—he's got everything, including the know-how to turn that piece of paper—like Cinderella's Fairy Godmother turning the pumpkin into a golden coach—into a five-million-dollar credit in a numbered Swiss bank account by tonight. And all records of the process lost—by laundering."

"How does he do that?" asked Bunbury, for whom the ins and outs of high finance forever remained a mystery.

"I don't know," confessed O'Leary. "But he's charging us 20 per cent commission on the deal. And that's cheap rate because I once did *him* a favour."

Bunbury flagged a passing waitress for more coffee. "When do we see this—friend?" he asked.

"At nine-thirty—in exactly three-quarters of an hour," replied the other. "Leadenhall Street, just as soon as his doors open. And then we make for the wide open spaces. Where do you fancy, Horace? I've decided on India."

Bunbury looked at his companion in some surprise. For one thing, it had not occurred to him that the pair of them were immediately going to split up after the con, for somehow—despite their small differences, the fact that the other had always treated him like a junior partner, and not forgetting the affair of the previous night—he, a basically friendless person, had come to take O'Leary's presence for granted. And the other surprising thing: it was the first time his companion had ever addressed him by his given name—to which he must make a small correction.

"My mother insisted on naming me Horace as a joke against my father, whom she didn't like very much," he said. "But at school I was always called Horse. After the Disney character Horace Horsecollar," he explained.

"Horse it is, then," responded O'Leary. "And I think it's high time you called me Tom." He looked at his watch. "Now, as soon as we've finished our coffee, I propose we drift over to Leadenhall Street and officially put ourselves in the millionaire class in time for dinner."

There were a couple of small attendant difficulties in the way of arriving at the friend's merchant bank: for one thing, half the road was up in Leadenhall Street, so their taxi was obliged to take a detour, in the course of which their driver got himself irremediably stuck in a traffic jam. The conspirators paid him off and walked the rest of the way, arriving at the door of the bank to find it shut, and with a uniformed constable of the City police on guard outside.

"Closed, sir," said the latter, as O'Leary essayed to try the handle.

"Really—why?" demanded the Irishman.

The constable pointed to a discreet notice—scarcely bigger than a visiting-card—that was pinned by the letter-box:

> *Closed by order of*
> *The Board of Trade*

Without a word, O'Leary took his companion by the arm and led him swiftly—but not too swiftly—away. When they had rounded a corner out of sight of the arm of the law, they stopped. Bunbury stared at O'Leary; the other looked keenly about him.

"What's happened, Tom?" whispered Bunbury.

"Trouble, at a guess," replied the other. "I'll ring up and find out. Ah, there's a phone box—come on!"

Jammed in the phone box together, Bunbury felt his stomach give a distinct and queasy roll as he watched the other dial a number.

"Hello, is that Sir Walter Tite's residence?" asked O'Leary at length. "Yes, who's that? Ah—is Sir Walter available to speak to Thomas O'Leary, please?

"What did you say?

"Good God, man—don't tell me this!" Bunbury distinctly saw him pale.

"When, man—*when?*"

A longish pause, as someone spoke at the other end. And then O'Leary slowly replaced the receiver.

"Your friend's dead," said Bunbury, with a stroke of intuition.

"Shot himself late last night," said the other. "That was the butler. He found him. The law must have got on to some of his rackets."

"I'm—terribly sorry, old chap," said Bunbury.

"We weren't—not really friends. But it comes as a shock. And it puts you and me in one hell of a hole."

They walked out into the busy morning street, past all the City gentlemen, the typists, clerks, messengers: an upturned anthill of disparate activities.

"What now?" asked Bunbury. "Why not fly to Switzerland and see what luck we have at doing a deal of our own with one of the Zurich numbered-account banks?"

O'Leary looked at him with something approaching admiration. "That's half-way to being a good idea, Horse," he declared. "In any event, it's one helluva lot better than sitting on our butts in London and waiting for the whole thing to blow up in our faces—as, on this morning's record, it's likely to do at any time."

The first travel agency they came across had people practically queueing up in the street outside to get in. They managed to fight their way to the counter, where a harassed clerk, sizing them up as better dressed and more articulate and incisive than the common ruck, gave them what was left of his full attention after the demands that two telephones—one tucked under each ear—made upon him.

"Yessir? (Just a moment, please.) Can I help you?"

"Two single tickets to Zurich—first class," said O'Leary.

"Nothing to Zurich."

"Somewhere along the way—Strasbourg?"

"No seats for the Continent today—or tonight."

"Oh, for Pete's sake—why not?"

"Haven't you heard? The dock strike's spread and the airlines are inundated with panic holiday traffic. (Hello, sir. Yes, I'm attending to your little problem.) I suggest you try again tomorrow."

"We don't have any tomorrow," cried O'Leary with commendable exaggeration. "Do you not have seats for anywhere in Europe?"

This put the clerk on his imaginative mettle: he rummaged around in a folder for a while and produced . . .

"Two tickets—return tourist—for Reykjavik. Take off at eighteen hundred hours."

There followed a muttered conversation between the two conspirators.

"What do you think, Tom?"

"Have you ever tried to launder a five-million-dollar cheque drawn on a New York bank—*in Iceland?* The bleeding penguins would laugh at you!

"Forget it!"

Breakfast-time in the penthouse apartment on the seventh floor of a cinema and restaurant complex off Tottenham Court Road was a movable feast. The Man, fresh from a two-year stretch in the Scrubs with the concomitant elegances of slopping out and breakfast in the half-light of early morning, found it difficult to sleep till noon—and would do so for several weeks till he had returned to his habitual hedonistic existence.

On this particular morning, he was lying in his Louis XVIII bed overlooking the indoor swimming pool and addressing himself to grilled Scotch kippers when Weasel Jilkes was announced on the intercom from the armoured entrance lobby below. It was barely nine-thirty.

"Well?" The Man picked up a fillet of kipper and chawed the delicate flesh from the slippery skin, melted butter and fish oil dribbling down his chin and soiling the Chinese dressing-gown that encased his massive torso. "Did ya do for O'Leary?"

Jilkes writhed inside his flashy suiting, cracked his bony knuckles, and looked up at the ceiling, as if for inspiration.

"I—I dunno what reely happened, boss," he ventured.

"You dunno what happened?" echoed the Man. "Well, if *you* dunno—who *do?*"

"We located the Irish bastard, boss," Jilkes began again.

"He was located *days* ago!" interposed his boss. "So what kept ya till now? Did ya do for him?"

"We got on the blower to him, like what you said, boss. Told him as how you was wanting to let bygones be bygones like. Then me and the boys waited in the Roller round the corner while Darkie, he went on up, to talk terms with O'Leary. Half an hour ago, and we wuz still waiting, but no Darkie. No nuffin."

The Man tossed the kipper skin aside and wiped his hands on the skirt of his dressing-gown. "Wuz Darkie carrying a shooter?" he demanded.

"I told him to," replied Weasel Jilkes, "but he wuz for doing O'Leary with his bare hands, like what he always does."

The Man nodded. "Never knew Darkie fail with his bare hands," he conceded. "Big as they came, he'd wring their necks like they wuz chickens. So then—he done for that Irish bastard, but you ain't seen him since—right?"

Jilkes writhed and looked uncomfortable again. "It ain't— quite like that, boss," he ventured.

The other's close-set eyes fixed on his henchman. "Then how is it?" he demanded.

"We ain't seen Darkie, boss," came the reply. "But O'Leary checked out of the hotel, baggage and all, at half-past eight— along with a new guy he's teamed up with. We found that out half an hour ago."

The Man's eyes swivelled towards his henchman. "What new guy's this?" he demanded. "Another Mick?"

"Not a Mick, boss. An English guy. A toff. They checked into the hotel at the same time and shared a room. We didn't see hair nor hide of the toff last night, but he left alonger O'Leary this morning at half-past eight, like we wuz told."

A long silence followed this announcement, and Weasel Jilkes shrank within his skin for fear of his boss's fury.

Presently the fury was unleashed. From the coarse mouth there issued a string of vile invective, the more vile because it was delivered in the high-pitched and androgynous voice that fitted so ill with his massive frame.

"Aaaah—what've I done to deserve you shmucks? That Darkie—he gets orders to go in and rub out a guy. All he has to do is sweet-talk him for a little while, then wring his neck when he's in the middle of a big laugh. So what does Darkie do?

"He goes and gets himself lost!"

He paced up and down the room, uneasily watched by his henchman.

"O'Leary—O'Leary!" piped the Man. "Everywhere I hear that name. In the Scrubs, all I hear is that name. And what is he? Nuffing but a bleedin' amateur! A bleedin' amateur! A poncey, lah-di-da amateur *and* a Mick!

"I ain't never met him socially—ya know why? I simply ain't good enough for the likes of he! The rest of the big-shots I mix with—Flash Jackie Noggs—Razor Creech—Morrie Spender, and all the rest—he ain't got no time for them, either. Not lah-di-da enough for Mister Mick O'Leary! None of us ain't!"

He stopped in his restless striding; pointed straight at the shrinking Weasel.

"Find him! Look for him where he hangs out—St. James's and all the toffee-nosed clubs where the lah-di-da geezers hang out. The West End hotels. Watch Ascot, Henley Regatta, Buckingham Palace garden parties.

"Find him—find him—FIND HIM!"

To underscore his intent, the Man picked up a very nice little Dresden shepherdess of porcelain and threw it at the far wall. He seemed to subside a little after that.

"Find him," he said in a quieter voice, thin and androgynous still. "For what he done to me, he's gotter go. While that lah-di-da bastard's still alive, I can't hold my head up wiv the geezers what matter in this town."

"We are in something of a cleft stick," announced O'Leary.

They were seated at a table outside a pub in a pleasant palazzo close by St. Paul's, where lightly clad tourists sauntered through, scattering truncated phrases, like confetti, in half the tongues of the world. It was sublimely hot. Bunbury was sucking orange and lemonade through a straw and envying his companion the Campari soda that he sipped at so appreciatively; for the first time since his "cure," he craved a real drink.

"We certainly are," conceded Bunbury. "And how do we get out of it? I mean—stuck here in Britain with a hot cheque we seem to be able to do nothing with. And, by the way, what would happen if I simply walked into my High Street bank and deposited it?"

"For a start, it would take a week or more for them to clear a U.S. cheque," said O'Leary, "during which time the manager of the High Street bank in question would have bent himself double trying to find out who you *really* were, what you *really* do for a living, and—implicitly—how in the hell you came by that cheque. Nothing makes quite such a brouhaha as five million smackers. And we can't afford that kind of noise!"

"What happens," asked Bunbury, "if Sawtry rings up the Crown Agents—say—this morning, and gives his instructions about the disposal of the monument?" He eyed his companion with head on one side. "Answer me that."

"You're right, we'd be done for," said O'Leary. "So he's got to be stopped—right now."

"How?"

"The Crown Agents—that's to say we—have got to go to *him*. Today. This morning. Now. Call it after-sales service. We've got to take his instructions—and go through the motions of making him think we're carrying 'em out."

Bunbury got to his feet, pushing aside his half-finished soft drink as he did so.

"What are we waiting for, then?" he demanded. "Next stop the Ritz. Come on!"

"Come on"—he heard himself say it, and enjoyed a slight frisson.

Alice ordering the duchess around!

For a week or more, the keen-eyed servitors in the echoing ground-floor halls of the Ritz Hotel had remarked upon the distinguished-looking American gentleman who habitually took a table facing the elevator around bar opening time at eleven in the morning, went in for luncheon at one-thirty, sat through till it was time to partake of an excellent tea at the same, or a nearby table, in the hall—and left around six. This was his routine, had been for over a week, and varied not at all. Most of the time, he was half-hidden behind a newspaper— either *The Wall Street Journal* or *The Times* of London. He always settled his bills in notes of the highest denominations and was a generous tipper. No one knew his name.

As to appearance, the stranger looked around the early to mid-thirties, with a good shock of dark hair, excellent complexion and physique, tall and slender in the right places, broad where it mattered. Dressed in suits and casuals of West End cut, hand-made shoes, and other details that are a give-away to staff in top service. Right out of the top drawer, inferred the knowledgeable: Ivy League and probably Oxbridge; professional—or richly leisured.

No one noticed—so discreetly well was it done—that the newspaper was also doubling for a screen that the American used like the masks of eighteenth-century Venetian gallants out on the town to espy likely conquests, nor that his prime interest appeared to be the women who emerged from the lift. It was, therefore, not to be expected that anyone noticed his most particular attention was always reserved for one woman. And she was invariably accompanied by her husband—at least, she was with her husband on every occasion save one. And that was a week or more after the stranger started upon his odd tryst at the Ritz.

It happened one mid-morning. One eye just peering over the top corner of his newspaper, the watcher saw *her* come out of the elevator—alone—and walk sedately across the suave carpeting that led past his chair in the direction of the revolving door.

Still retaining the newspaper as a shield, he continued covertly to watch her till she was nearly abreast of him, and then without warning leapt to his feet and greeted her with a glad cry—as if he had been expecting her.

"Darling! I thought you'd forgotten the day—the time—the place!"

And then he just—looked—at her.

"I think you'd better sit down," he murmured in quite a different tone of voice. "If you passed out from shock, the neighbours might talk."

Obediently she took the seat opposite him, staring at him in total fascination mixed with alarm. She licked her dry lips; somehow she steadied herself and murmured, "Have you got a cigarette?"

"Sure." He produced a combined case and lighter in gold: provided her and lit her, and his darkly smouldering eyes never left her face.

"You're looking fine, real fine, Daisy. Married life suits you. I always said that, didn't I?"

She exhaled a lungful of smoke and regarded him through it.

"What are you doing here?" she whispered.

He spread his hands in a mock gesture of injured innocence. "Now, is that the way to talk to your ever-loving who you haven't seen in four years? Four years! I could forgive your regrettable lapse of memory, but—"

"What lapse of memory?" she snapped. "What are you trying to put over on me now?"

He smiled a feline smile. "I refer to the tiny little fact that you should have taken out and refurbished before you trotted up the aisle the other week, baby—but which somehow got hidden away in a dark corner of your sweet mind and covered all over in cobwebs.

"I refer to the fact that you were already married to yours sincerely, and still are!—*Mrs.* George G. Sawtry!"

The brunette whom he had earlier addressed as Daisy stabbed out the cigarette with shaking fingers. "What do you want with me, Zachary?" she demanded. "Tell me that—and then go away and leave me alone."

He grinned to show a perfect mouth of teeth—all his own.

"Your approach, like always, darling, is pleasantly direct, but a little crude," he said.

"I didn't have your many advantages," she retorted. "Like, I wasn't brought up by a crazy old witch of a grandmother who'd once been an upstairs maid in some millionaire's mansion on Bellevue Avenue, and who filled your head full of ideas about being a gentleman."

He smiled sidelong at her, most beguilingly, and stroked the side of his cheek. "And I turned out a gentleman, just like Grandma wanted, didn't I?"

"A gentleman with the mind of a sewer rat!" she retorted. "Which got you sent up the river for life," she added. "So how in the hell do you come to be here? You couldn't have been paroled, not after only four years. Not for what you did."

He flicked a piece of invisible dust from the knee of his well-pressed grey slacks. "I was sprung," he said. "It cost me, along with travelling money and new duds, every penny of the Kansas City heist I had stashed away. And all for you, darling—just to come and see my little wife, who'd decided to fill in the thirty years' waiting time for yours sincerely by getting herself hitched to a multimillionaire."

She leaned forward and responded savagely, almost spitting out the words, "Then go home, sucker! There's nothing in this for you!"

He clicked his tongue and shook his head. "Tch, tch, there's gratitude for you. And all I'm looking for is a little hospitality from you and Mr. Sawtry. Like a suite alongside yours right here in the Ritz. Just somewhere to stay while I finalize my plans."

"What plans?" she demanded.

"I have in mind to have a little plastic surgery by one of the top London men at the game," he said. "Then I thought a world cruise might help blow away the everlasting stink of that little pad in cell block eighteen that I shared with two other guys for four years. After that—oh, I thought I might go into business somewhere in Europe. I've got a very open mind. You know me, babe."

"You've got me written in as a meal ticket," she said.

"That's right, Daisy honey." He smiled. "Pleasantly direct, as ever. And there isn't a thing you can do about it. If I blow the whistle on you, the limeys will deport you, and you'll be facing a federal rap for aiding and abetting an escaped convict beside which the charge of bigamy will be merely picayune, a side-dish.

"So play it cool, Daisy sweetie. Do your piece for your long-lost cousin Zach and cousin Zach will play ball along with you.

"By the way, do you have any folding money there in your handbag?"

"I—a little," she answered, eyeing him in trepidation, with a trembling nether lip—as she had done since he laid his cards on the table.

"Give it to me." He held out his hand, and she passed him a slim fold of banknotes, which he counted.

"Fifty lousy pounds!" he complained. "Does George G. Sawtry enjoy you on the cheap, kid? It wasn't like this when you were hustling in the old days."

"I have charge accounts almost everywhere," she said, "and my credit cards. That's just for taxis and things like that.

"Listen, Zachary . . ."

"I'm all ears and eyes, babe," he purred.

"I'll go along with you, but—can't we get this thing over quickly? One straight cheque made out to you, to cover all you need. I can fix this quite easily on my personal account, and my husb . . . George will never even know about it. What do you say?"

Before replying, he hailed a waiter and fixed drinks for them both; later, over the rim of his glass, he enjoyed the sight of her squirming with suspenseful anticipation of his reply to her proposition.

The reply, when it came, was unequivocal. "No to that, kid," he said. "I am in no hurry. Four years in one place disposes a guy to let a little time go by in such deals as the one I propose.

"We'll do it my way. You will introduce me to your 'husb . . . George' as long-lost cousin Zachary, late of Bellevue Avenue, Newport, Rhode Island. You will then fix me up in an adjoining suite and we will let a little time go by." He leered at her. "I haven't come all this way just for a meal-ticket, Daisy honey. Four years is a long time to sit around thinking about one's little wifie. . . ."

He reached out and touched her hand; so appalled was the self-styled Mrs. Desirée Sawtry that she did not immediately snatch it away.

"While a little time goes by, we'll make some time, mmm? Just like in the old days."

"I was wrong about you, Zachary Colenso," she said. "You're not a sewer rat—compared with you, a sewer rat has some style. You are a common louse! And my name's now Desirée!"

He grinned. "Yup—but I'm the common louse who's calling all the shots.

"Desirée—nice! Pretty name for a hooker who finally made good."

SIX

Bunbury and O'Leary had only to announce themselves at the desk and a message came down: would they go right on up to Mr. Sawtry's suite?

"Gentlemen, I was just about to call you at your office," declared Sawtry as they entered his elegantly furnished drawing-room. "What'll you have, fellers? Forgive the informality: I feel I've known you for years."

He wrung their hands fervently; they exchanged secret glances at the narrowness of their escape.

Over drinks (lime juice for Bunbury), Sawtry expounded his needs.

"I want for the memorial to be over in Texas and re-erected at my ranch by my wife's birthday on October fourth," he declared. "Now, fellers—give me your reactions to that."

"Early October doesn't give us a lot of time, sir," said O'Leary. "Judd and I have been working out the logistics on the dismantling, and we can't bring it down to less than four weeks at the most. Crating and transportation—and if you want the memorial erected by October the fourth, the whole thing will have to go by air freight—another two weeks. Then there's re-erection on the site—another month at least. I just don't see it in the time. Check, Judd?"

"Agreed," said Bunbury, and did some totally meaningless sums on a pocket calculator which, anticipating their line of approach, they had stopped off to buy on the way to the Ritz. "I don't see the operation completed, the Albert Memorial re-erected in Texas, before the end of the year"—he stabbed at the buttons of the calculator with all the meaningless expertise of a movie actor playing the role of Chopin—"December the twenty-third earliest, twenty-ninth latest." He sat back from the keyboard and waited for the audience's applause.

To the conspirators' surprise, Sawtry sat back and smiled almost benignly. "Gentlemen, I had anticipated your reply," he said. "The demand I made upon you was my top requirement, which, in all fairness, I knew to be on the unreasonable side.

"However, I have a compromise proposal to make." His smile faded, his expression grew stern, and one realized at a glance why it is that the Indians no longer rule the great plains of Texas.

"And what is that, sir?" asked O'Leary.

Before answering, Sawtry pressed a button on the table beside him and almost immediately three men issued from the door behind Bunbury's chair; turning, he saw three of the biggest and toughest-looking Western types he had ever encountered outside the flea-pit picture theatre that he used to frequent during his school holidays. All were wearing Western-style hats, the one in the middle—the biggest—an item of headgear known to fame as a "ten-gallon."

"I should like you to meet my henchmen, gentlemen," said Sawtry in what could only be described as faintly menacing tones. "In the centre is my foreman, Tex Manacle. Flanking him on left and right respectively are Duke Dakota and Chuck Dangerfield."

Introductions effected, the trio remained standing where they were and the conference was resumed—but under the faint cloud of menace that had entered with the cowboys.

"Gentlemen, you will recall the group of statuary positioned at the north-western end of the memorial complex," said Sawtry. "It depicts the something or other of America—the word evades me."

"Apotheosis?" suggested Bunbury.

"The very word. I thank you," said the other. "Now, this particular fragment of the whole, this apotheosis, struck me—speaking as an American, a patriot, and also as a member of the human race—most forcibly, as indeed it struck my little wife on the occasion that I took her to see the memorial and pointed out some of the finer features.

"My compromise proposal, gentlemen, is that you begin work on the Albert Memorial by detaching the *America* group from the whole, crating it up, and delivering same to Heathrow in very good time for me to arrange onward transportation and re-erection at my ranch well before—I would say two weeks before—my wife's birthday."

"Now, I expect you to agree that this is a reasonable compromise." He smiled, and it was a thin, vulpine smile entirely lacking in the warmth of humour. "But, reasonable or not, I shall expect the crate or crates to be at Heathrow in one week from now."

Bunbury experienced a sinking feeling within him; it was O'Leary who reacted first.

"Sir, you mistake our problem," he said. And it seemed to Bunbury that his companion in crime was almost literally driving by the seat of his pants and ad-libbing his arguments off the top of his head, and he was full of admiration for him in consequence. "Our problem, whether in dismantling the whole of, or part of, the monument, remains the same: the erection of scaffolding and the preliminaries to the operation will take at least two days in either case. That doesn't leave much time out of a week."

George G. Sawtry's eyes narrowed. . . .

"That statuary group is going to be crated up at Heathrow seven days from today," he said. "Ain't that so, Tex?" he added, addressing his foreman.

The latter took a couple of paces forward and, laying one hairy, bear-like paw on Bunbury's shoulder (but as gently as any mother touching her baby's head), growled in his ear, "You heard what the boss said, bud. One week you got. So why are you sittin' around on your fat butt doin' nothin' right now?"

To give George G. Sawtry his due, his Draconian demand was entirely due to the current transport strike, which had dislocated sea and air services throughout Great Britain, had spread to the Continent, and even put tremendous pressure on the transatlantic route. Sawtry had won a lien on an air freighter to New York on the day in question—the last forseeable opportunity to get part of Desirée's present home in time for her birthday.

The multimillionaire did not trouble to justify his action to "Dr. Judd and Colonel Abey"—and, anyhow, these two worthies were already out of the Ritz Hotel and looking for a quiet spot where they could figure out what the hell to do next to defend their hard-won five million dollars.

After tea that same day, Rosalind Purvis took out the small electric grass cutter and went over the tiny lawn of the bijou *cottage orné*. She was presently buttonholed by her friend Hannah, who, returning from work, sought out the other and faced up to a certain situation in her customary direct manner.

"Roz, why have you been avoiding me?"

The other, though in every respect a worthy, honest person, jibbed away from such a challenge—as most people do.

"I haven't been avoiding you, Han," she lied, switching off the mower.

"Who got up early, made herself a cup of coffee, and then went back to bed and stayed there till I'd gone out?" challenged the other.

"It signified nothing."

"Who was simply not to be seen all day yesterday?"

"All right—I've been busy around the house."

A pause, and . . .

"Too busy, perhaps, to follow up the business of the phoney Major Arbuthnot?"

"Why do you go on about that, Han?"

"Because I'm your friend and because I don't like to see you being made a fool of," said Hannah. "And even though your job with the Walbrook's purely voluntary and unpaid, I wouldn't like you to be thrown out of it in disgrace. That's why I go on about it."

"Well, if you must know," said Rosalind, "I haven't done

anything about—about the person in question. Not yet, I haven't."

Hannah deliberately counted up to three. "And when *are* you going to blow the whistle on that flagrant crook?" she demanded.

"When I've—when I've made further enquiries."

"What further enquiries?"

"We-e-eell—there's the builder whom I also met," said Rosalind. "I told you about him. He will be worth questioning, to give me a lead to Major Arbuthnot."

"Yes, you told me about him," conceded Hannah. "Clegg, Jr., of Clegg and Sons, Builders, Balham. Well, dear, following up that particular lead shouldn't exercise your ingenuity too much. If you check the phone book—as I did—you'll find there's no such firm as Clegg and Sons, either in Balham or elsewhere."

"Then I suppose I'd better go to the police," said Rosalind, with what sounded like meek resignation.

"And also write a report to the Walbrook," prompted Hannah. "In case they find out first that you've been duped."

"I'll do that," promised Rosalind. "Just as soon as I've finished cutting the lawn."

She switched on the machine and went off down the narrow swath of green, watched by her friend.

Hannah shook her head ruefully.

The following day, the attached letter appeared on the desk of a fairly junior clerk at the Ancient Monuments and Historic Buildings Directorate. It was from the Department of the Environment, the titular overlord of the AM&HBD, and was signed by the private secretary to the Secretary of State himself. The headed writing paper—though the junior clerk would never have dreamed of questioning such a thing—was not genuine, but an excellent facsimile.

The contents were such that he filed away the missive and forgot it; which was a pity, because had he been of a busybody-ish disposition he could have earned for himself a small piece

of immortality, along with certain promotion that—unhappily
—was ever to evade him.

TO: **DEPARTMENT OF THE ENVIRONMENT**
Ancient Monuments   2 Marsham Street, SW1P 3EB
& Historic Buildings   Tel: (01) 212 3434
Directorate
(Department A.)   Date as postmark

Sirs,
The Secretary of State wishes me to inform you that a Certain
Member of the Royal Family has commented on the dingy
appearance of the Prince Consort National Memorial (popu-
larly known as The Albert Memorial), and since the exalted
Personage in question, like many gentlemen of the naval per-
suasion, is particularly sensitive to smartness & cleanliness, the
Secretary of State (who was present at the time) immediately
ordered the matter to be put right.

This letter, therefore, is to inform you that the DOE has
commissioned Messrs. Duckworth, Todd & Company to wash
down the memorial. The work will commence tomorrow. The
AM&HBD will not concern themselves with the matter, and
the account will be settled from central funds.

In view of the frequently derogatory comments which, to
the distress of the Royal Family, the monument excites in both
the popular and the architectural presses, there will be no
publicity hand-outs related to the cleansing, which should take
one week only.

     Yours faithfully,

           [Signed]

The above fruit of the conspirators' combined ingenuity,
which they had together concocted, printed, and typed in the
bedroom of their new billet in the Strand, and posted in the
late collection, was but an elegant preliminary to the effort of
assembling men and materials to fulfil the promise of the letter. This took them all night and most of the following forenoon. It was not till gone 11 a.m. that a motley collection of

lorries and delivery vans appeared in Kensington Gore and, parking right opposite the Albert Memorial, were unloaded of scaffolding poles and attachments, huge sheets of translucent heavy-duty plastic, coils upon coils of rubber hose, brushes, shovels, scrapers, buckets, innumerable boxes of indeterminate gear. And six workmen plus the two conspirators.

The transport unloaded, the vehicles took their departure. Within five minutes, watched anxiously by Bunbury and O'Leary, the scaffolding erectors had already set up their foundations and were preparing to raise a skeleton of tubular steel poles from ground level to the cross that surmounted the edifice 180 feet above. Simultaneously, the three other workmen—the cleaners—were laying out their hoses and connecting the master end to a fire hydrant nearby.

By this time, two contractors' notice-boards had been attached to the edifice. The first was legitimate advertising matter for a perfectly legitimate firm:

J. Poulter
Scaffolding
Tel: 199 3435

The second was a conceit knocked up by Bunbury and O'Leary to add—in the phrase of W. S. Gilbert—"corroborative detail, intended to give artistic verisimilitude":

Duckworth, Todd & Company
Monumental Cleaners & Restorers
By Appointment
Telephone: 207 4444 (10 lines)

The two conspirators were disparately dressed for the occasion: Bunbury in a useful-looking sports jacket with leather patches at the elbows, narrow-cut cavalry twill slacks, a cheese-cutter cap: very much the young milord checking up to see how the chaps were getting along with restoring the south wing of the family seat. By contrast, O'Leary was in legal-clerical grey, bowler hat, brief-case, rolled umbrella, Guards tie: the complete city gent in full-dress uniform.

"I'm off then, Horse," said the latter. "Good luck to you today, and whatever happens I know you'll do your best to keep the ball in the air. If you come unstuck, cut and run—but first of all throw away the Duckworth, Todd notice-board. When I come back, I'll cruise past in a taxi, and if I see the board's gone, I'll know the game is up."

They shook hands: it was Verey lights over the Western Front, the tac-tac of machine-guns from the Boche trenches opposite, the two gallant young officers making their last farewells before going over the top.

"And good luck to you with that five-million cheque, Tom," said Bunbury. "Pull off the laundering trick and we'll be in France tomorrow, even if we have to hire a boat and row across!"

By late afternoon, the erection crew, by near-superhuman efforts, had raised the scaffolding and covered the entire lattice-work of steel with the translucent plastic sheeting, which served efficiently to hide the activities within the carapace from the prying eyes of the general public or from anyone else. The three erectors then had the British workman's traditional brew-up of tea and departed—leaving Bunbury and the three "cleaners," who had thus far done no more than connect up their hoses and permit a generous deluge of water to cascade down over the noble bronze brow of Albert the Good, divide into a dozen mini waterfalls over his lap, and descend by way of his Garter cloak, knee breeches, and pumps to the floor of the monument, and then on down the steps and out into the gutter—thereby demonstrating to outsiders who might have been in doubt that the Prince Consort National Memorial was, indeed, being washed down—in the terms of the letter to the AM&HBD, purporting to have come from the DOE.

The genuine workmen having departed, Bunbury reviewed the three remaining. All had done service during the memorable reception and auction at the Plantagenet Hotel, and all had behaved themselves not too badly by the standards of that evening. There was Dickie Duveen, a former juvenile lead who had been something of a matinée idol till Anno Domini and avoirdupois overcame him; booze and a general disinclination to effort had completed the transformation and brought him to his present state, which was that of a fat, jolly layabout who, considering his misfortunes, added his small bit to the sum of human happiness by being unflaggingly cheerful in all circumstances. There was Norman D'Arcy, not of the legitimate theatre, but once an illusionist, in the course of which he made a great deal of money and enjoyed a considerable éclat by sawing a lady in half on-stage—till something went wrong with the act and he made a ghastly mistake; it says much for D'Arcy's character that he gave all his savings to the distraught widower of the lady in question, and never touched a saw again. Lastly, there was Hugo Horowicz, once a baritone of some distinction till the demon drink turned him, like so many others, into a bad investment for impresarios; Horowicz's last public appearance had, fortuitously, been at the last night of the Proms when, at the close of his aria, he fell off the stage of the Royal Albert Hall and into the arms of the front row of cheering student promenaders; now he was playing another role just across the way from the scene of his final disaster—but, let it be said, also of some previous triumphs.

This, then, was the raw material that Bunbury surveyed as they paraded before him under the tabernacle of the great monument, in the unearthly light provided by the all-enveloping plastic.

The trio already knew the broad outlines of the con (how could they not, having attended the auction?), but not the late developments, save that they were pretending to wash down the monument as a cover for doing something entirely different.

Bunbury proceeded to brief them as to what they were really about.

"What we're going to do, chaps," he began, "is to prepare this statuary group"—pointing to *America*—"for removal and crating up in sections. I shall be marking out the lines on the stonework where, later this week, we shall saw the figures up into fairly portable pieces—"

"Saw—did you say *saw?*" interjected Norman D'Arcy. "Through *stone?*"

"It's really quite simple," replied Bunbury. "Given the right kind of stone-slicing saw—which will be provided."

"Well, all right—if you say so," said D'Arcy, former sawyer, doubtfully.

"Meanwhile," continued Banbury, "I want you chaps to start removing some of these blocks of stone"—he pointed to the upper part of the surround of the plinth upon which the statuary group was resting—"so that when the time comes for a crane to do the lifting, we can get our slings underneath.

"Got that? Any questions?"

There being no questions, or any dissension (save a certain amount of head-shaking by D'Arcy, who, with his expert knowledge of other media, was doubtful about sawing through stone), the trio set to with hammers and cold chisels and worked diligently till their quitting time at 5:30 P.M.

Bunbury wished them a good evening, reminding them to be on time (8:30) in the morning, and watched the three ill-matched former show-business people stroll away into the summery quiet of Kensington Gore, no doubt in search of a suitable public house that would be opening at six. He was alone in the plastic-girt monument, now more like a mausoleum, with the grave-faced Albert looking down at him from his canopied throne.

Not a man given to excess of imagination, nor to morbid thoughts of death and dissolution, Bunbury was curiously moved, that warm summer's early evening, to be standing in that towering cathedral of stone, iron, and plastic sheeting. The noise of traffic moving up and down Kensington Gore was muted to a far-off murmur, the most insistent sound being that of the plastic sheeting as it flapped gently in the passing zephyrs, like the sails of a ship becalmed in the horse latitudes.

He felt sufficiently moved to look up and address the heroic-sized bronze; this he did in a whisper that oddly reverberated about him.

"Your Royal Highness, I don't want you to worry, because everything's going to be perfectly all right, that I promise you. Your memorial will survive long after all the glass and concrete monstrosities have gone and been forgotten, and folks are building again like they used—for love, for faith, for fun. . . ."

A handclap behind him; turning, he saw O'Leary. The Irishman's face was lit up with a heartening grin.

"Well spoken," he said. "That was a glimmer of truth and sanity that warms my cheerless day."

"You haven't scored with the cheque," said Bunbury, and it was not a question.

The other shook his head, took off his bowler, and settling himself down on the flagstones with his back to Prince Albert's plinth, unfastened his hand-made shoes and took them off with a sigh.

"I have not," he said. "All morning I spent in the City, traipsing from one merchant bank to the next, following up hunches and gone-cold leads, half-forgotten friendships and broken dreams. Man, every time I mentioned a five-million-dollar cheque drawn on a New York bank, you'd think I'd brought in the Crown Jewels with the blood of the Tower garrison still upon them!

"Lunch-time, I betook me to St. James's, to the best of clubland, and there I gatecrashed the citadels of privilege, blarneying the keepers of the gates with stories of being the luncheon guest of a distinguished member; buttonholing fellers at the bar with whom I had a slight acquaintance. All to no use.

"I'd have braved the Cavalry and Guards, but the shadow of disgrace still hangs over me there—and me a poor orphan boy from County Cork." From the hip pocket of his immaculate trousers he withdrew a silver hip-flask and took a swig, grimaced, turned the vessel upside down and watched sadly as the last few drops thinly splattered a paving stone.

"It's only your first day on the job," ventured Bunbury by way of consolation. "And we've all week."

"The trouble with this con," said O'Leary. "You know wha' the trouble with this con is, my dear Horse?"

"No, tell me."

"We asked for too much moolah. Now, if we'd settled for less, we'd be in clover. That's the irony of it.

"If we'd let the mark have Albert for a cool quarter of a million, we'd be sitting pretty by now. We could even be in Reykjavik!" He lay back in paroxysms of helpless mirth.

He was drunker than he looked. Bunbury helped him down into a taxi and they were driven back to their hotel. Only once on the way did O'Leary give proof that his agile mind was by no means completely eclipsed.

"I rang the mark from the City," he said. "Told him that we'd got started on the job and everything was fine. He said he'd be along tomorrow to inspect."

"Oh no!" groaned Bunbury.

"Oh yes. And you'd better see to it that those three clowns you've got working for you are hard at it and not playing leap-frog."

The taxi slid through Trafalgar Square and up into the Strand. O'Leary opened his eyes again. "I wouldn't have you think," he said, "that I wasted any time today. By the time I left the City, there was only me, a stray dog, and several pieces of paper blowing about the empty streets."

"You did a great job," said Bunbury. "And you'll do even better tomorrow."

The second day of what the conspirators had come to refer to as the "two-pronged effort," O'Leary went straight off to the City, where he had already set up an appointment with the stringer of a Swiss bank who made quite encouraging noises over the phone, though as yet no amount had been quoted.

"When I mention five million, he'll remember that he has to dash off to another engagement," said O'Leary. He grinned.

"But I'll bring him down on the way to the door with a flying rugger tackle!" And in this positive mood, he departed.

It was with considerably less buoyancy that, later, Bunbury addressed himself to the task of clambering all over the *America* group in shirt-sleeves—no feat for the nervous, and he had no head for heights. His object was to determine how the figures could be sawn up into handy-sized chunks for transportation by air, and afterwards cemented together without the joins showing: it took some working out.

Dickie, Norman, and Hugo, meanwhile, though totally unused to and unfitted for any form of manual labour, had made fair inroads into removing the very sizeable pieces of facing stone from *America*'s plinth. That, together with the most professional-looking dotted lines on the "Cut Here" principle with which Bunbury had begun to embellish the group of apotheosized tenants of the plinth certainly gave the impression that real and determined action was intended.

It certainly struck George G. Sawtry that way when he arrived later on that morning with his entourage. . . .

"Great, great, Dr. Judd!" declared the Texan. "You guys of the Crown Agency are certainly versatile in your accomplishments." He gazed up at the manifest attributes of the Indian lady astride the buffalo. "And you say that this group can be re-erected intact in good time for"—he glanced sidelong at Desirée, who alone among his entourage appeared to be taking no interest in the proceedings—"in time for you-know-what?"

"Undoubtedly, sir," responded Bunbury. "And the joins won't show."

"Aaah—pardon me," said Sawtry, and he gestured to his entourage which, in addition to Desirée and his three cowboys, also included a most pleasant-looking man: handsome, well built, and expensively tailored, he made an exceedingly good initial impression on Bunbury. "Allow me to present my wife's cousin Mr. Zachary Colenso. Zach, I'd like for you to meet Dr. Judd of the British Crown Agents, who vended me this masterpiece."

The newcomer's hand-clasp was firm and sincere. "Glad to meet you, Doctor, I've heard quite a lot about you from George and Desirée," he said. "Great enterprise you've got here—to shift this edifice, stone by stone."

Sawtry looked towards his wife, who was staring absently into the middle distance. "Honey, come and look see how the boys are progressing," he said.

She moved over, gave the *America* group a disinterested glance, and said, "It's looking great, George. Now, if you don't mind, I'll take a cab and keep my appointment at the Health Club." She gave Bunbury a mechanical smile—the sort that some extraordinarily pretty women can produce the way a dog wags its tail.

"You do that, hon," responded her fond, innocent partner in bigamy. "A massage and a Jacuzzi will set you up real fine."

"I've been a little worried about cousin Desirée," interposed Colenso with some concern. "Maybe she hasn't been sleeping nights."

Bunbury thought he saw the lady in question throw a sudden glance of loathing at the author of this observation—but decided on balance that he must have imagined it.

Desirée departed, and they watched her go—the three ex-show-business characters included—and former matinée idol Dickie Duveen with a wistful sigh for days long gone.

"A great gal," declared George G. Sawtry. "Yes, a great gal!"

"But, speaking as her cousin," said Colenso, "I am a little worried for her. I'm sure she's overdoing it."

"You could be right at that, Zach," said Sawtry. He turned to Bunbury. "Zach is one helluva bright guy, you know. Explored up the Amazon. Lectured at Harvard and Oxford. Written books on subjects like I haven't even heard of the subjects." He gave the other a fond smile—the kind that men of mature years will bestow upon surrogates for the sons they never had. "When we get back home, I'm going to appoint him to vice-presidencies in a whole lot of my companies. To keep it in the family, y'know.

"I'm a great believer in—what's the word, Doctor?"

"Nepotism?" suggested Bunbury.

"The very word. I thank you."

"Hate him—I *hate* him!"

She spat out the words—aloud. The cab driver half turned his head in some alarm.

"What wuz that you said, lidy?" he cried.

"Nothing!"

Situated in a quiet mews close by Bond Street, Aphrodite's Health Club was the "in" place for faded and not so faded society beauties and visiting fireladies. Its fame had reached Desirée's circle in New York, and the strain to which she had been subjected since her "cousin's" arrival on the scene directed her footsteps to Aphrodite's the way a hart pants after the water brooks.

She was received by "Aphrodite" herself, a lady of indeterminate years, much advantaged by her own treatments and a lifetime of self-denial; she affected a Greek chiton and wore her ice-blonde hair in a high chignon—as befitted the personification of the goddess of love.

"An oil massage, I think, modom," she essayed, when she had viewed Desirée laid out nude on a replica of the altar to Diana at Ephesus. "Persephone," she said, addressing an acolyte, "will you please ask Hermione to give modom an oil massage in the Acropolis Room."

Desirée was carried in a litter to the Acropolis Room and laid upon a similar altar to the last. She had no more than a few moments to wait before another female acolyte entered, dressed in the costume of ancient Greece. But the remarkable thing was not the costume, the hair-do, or the pleasant manner with which the newcomer—she announced herself as Hermione—addressed her, but rather the springing between them of a mutual recognition: in hers, a certain astonishment and disbelief; in the other's, something very near to horrified alarm.

"Well, hello, Princess," said Desirée—the first to find her

voice. "We met the other evening at the Plantagenet Hotel, remember?

"But how come a nice girl like *Your Royal Highness* is working in a joint like this?"

SEVEN

The sight of the Albert Memorial covered entirely in plastic sheeting, and with a continuous torrent of water sluicing out of it and down the guttering of Kensington Gore, did not excite any great interest in Londoners, to whom the edifice was a familiar excrescence that one totally ignored: the tourists, on the other hand, simply wrote it out of their itineraries. Nor did the London press so much as obliquely allude to the washing down—and here kindly fate played into the hands of the conspirators, for the transport strike that had flashed through Britain like a bush-fire and was catching alight on the Continent relegated such humdrum items of local domesticity to oblivion.

On the evening of the next working day, Dickie, Norman, and Hugo had packed up and gone off on their evening pub crawl, leaving Bunbury and O'Leary to pick over the sorry rags of their present position and prospects; both position and prospects were unchanged.

"We must keep going," opined Bunbury stoutly. "Four to five days before the game's up. Ample time to pull something off, old man. How did it go today, anyhow?"

"Some of it—promising," replied O'Leary. "I have a clear lead to a character—a former M.P. who wisely ducked out from under when it got around that he was using the Palace of Westminster as an office for some very shady offshore deals— who is certainly *au fait* with the laundry business, but might well mulct us for anything up to 40 per cent, particularly if he figures that we're in a tight corner (and the fact that the cheque's dated three days ago and we still haven't banked it will give the cunning bastard some food for speculation). However, we're lunching at the Caprice tomorrow, and he knows roughly what my requirement is, so there won't be any beating about the bush. *And* he's picking up the tab."

They were lolling against *America*'s plinth, pleasantly refreshed by the enclosed space whose air had been cooled all that hot day by running water.

"Tell you what," said Bunbury. "Never did hear what became of the body of your friend Darkie whatsisname . . ."

"Darkie Todd," supplied O'Leary. He laughed briefly. "Wouldn't expect the discovery of the odd corpse in a train to make the headlines."

"Not even when he'd been murdered?" asked the other, eyeing his companion keenly.

O'Leary grinned and shook his head. "You've got a one-track mind in many regards," he said. "You still think I bumped off that guy, don't you?"

"Not necessarily," replied Bunbury cautiously.

"Well, I didn't," said O'Leary. "He went and died on me—a heart attack, I expect."

"How did it happen?"

"He knocked on our door. I was expecting him—the phone call, you know. Next up, the blighter was trying to break my neck. Damned near did, too—he had the strength of King Kong. Then, all of a sudden—woomph—he keeled over and fell. Stone cold dead and blue around the gills when I turned him over."

"But what was it all about?" demanded Bunbury. "Why the phone call, and why did he try to kill you?"

O'Leary may or may not have been about to answer his accomplice's demand there and then—one will never know.

A sound made them turn. . . .

"Well, we've got an unexpected visitor," said O'Leary. "Mrs. George G. Sawtry—what a pleasant surprise!"

She was dressed as she had been that morning when they saw her last, but was otherwise greatly changed; the strain had gone from her mouth and the tiredness from around her eyes. It might have been the beneficial ministrations she had received at the hands of Aphrodite's acolytes; she herself would have put it down to a psychological boost she had enjoyed that day.

"I've come to take you boys for a drink," was her surprising announcement.

Bunbury, slow on the uptake, glanced questioningly at his companion; O'Leary never questioned an offer—any offer—from a pretty woman.

"That's darned handsome of you, ma'am," he replied. "My colleague and I accept with much pleasure. Do you have transport?"

"Yes, I have," replied Desirée. "As a matter of fact, I bought me a little runabout only this afternoon. Nearly new. Quite cute."

The "little runabout," when they reached it (parked on a double yellow line, unscathed; there is a guardian angel who ministers exclusively to the requirements of rich, beautiful lady motorists), proved to be an Aston Martin Gran Turismo in racing green. Bunbury piled into the back and his companion took the passenger seat beside their glamorous driver.

"I'll take you to a cute pub I stumbled over the other evening when I was on the loose," she informed them. "Then, over drinks, I'll make you one of those classic propositions you won't be able to refuse."

It seemed to Bunbury, who was a mild aficionado of classic cars, that Desirée had scarcely time to change up and down through the gears before the Aston's magnificent engine had borne them, in some style, to a pleasant-looking pub in a quiet road at the back of Portland Square. Minutes later, they were seated at a rustic table in a leafy garden where Chinese lanterns—already lit in the early evening shadow and low-cast sun—hung from the branches of gnarled old trees.

"What'll you have?" asked she.

O'Leary called for Irish whiskey, Bunbury for a virgin Mary (which won him a raised eyebrow of surprise from their hostess), and she had a dry Martini.

"Your very good health, ma'am," they both murmured.

"Here's to you, boys," she responded. "And here's to—*crime.*"

A long, contemplative silence followed. . . .

"That was a great confidence trick you played on my husband," said Desirée without heat. "It beats me why you're still sticking around instead of beating the hell out of here."

"How did you know we . . . ?" began Bunbury—but stopped himself when he caught a warning look from his accomplice.

"Remember the resting actress who played Her Royal Highness at your charade the other night?" said Desirée. "Well, I ran across her today in her present role of masseuse. When challenged, she sang like a bird."

"But she didn't tell more than she knew," said O'Leary blandly, "and you're still deficient in the finer points of our present enterprise."

She smiled sweetly. "I still know enough to put you away for a long stretch unless you play ball," she retorted.

"What's the proposition?" asked O'Leary.

"Yes—the proposition?" echoed Bunbury.

Desirée snapped her fingers at a passing waitress and demanded a repeat order. She then crossed one shapely leg over the other and regarded her companions.

"Since it's a proposition you can't refuse and we are going to be in this thing together right up to our necks, I can square with you absolutely," she declared.

"Go on."

"Please continue."

"You met Zachary Colenso this morning, Dr. Judd."

"That's right," confirmed Bunbury. "Charming fellow. Your cousin, as I remember. Brilliant, so your husband was saying. Been everywhere, done everything."

"Been inside most of the top-grade penitentiaries in the States," replied Desirée. "Likewise done almost everything but grow mustard seed on his mother's grave for profit, or blow up the White House. Though I don't exclude the possibility of his having attempted both!

"And, for the record, he isn't my cousin. And I want him dead!" For graphic illumination of her requirement, she drew the heel of her palm across her throat.

Another thoughtful silence.

"I have to tell you, ma'am," said O'Leary. "We are strictly con men. Not hit men!"

"That's right!" confirmed Bunbury.

"There's no need for you to kill him," replied Desirée, "that's already taken care of. The proposition is that you dispose of the body, and in return I dummy up about your Albert Memorial con."

The two conspirators looked at each other questioningly; it was Bunbury who expressed what was in both their minds.

"Five million dollars which, if everyone had his own in this wicked world, would belong to your husband—you're willing to keep quiet about *that?*"

"Yes," replied Desirée. "To George Sawtry it's just a figure on a bank statement—nothing more."

"And just so that we'll dispose of a body?"

"That's right."

"Where do you figure we dump this body, Mrs. Sawtry?" asked O'Leary.

"Somewhere out of sight beneath the Albert Memorial— where else?" she replied. "Heaven sakes, you're not kidding me that you're *really* going to move that beautiful great hunk of stone anyplace!"

An exchange of glances, and the pair let that one go by.

"Um—where is the body now, ma'am?" essayed Bunbury.

"Still walking around and poisoning the air," responded Desirée. "On account of I haven't killed him yet."

The Man's existence—one could scarcely call it living—was of a simplicity (disregarding the superficial trappings of barbaric luxury that Sardanapalus might have thought to be a little over the top) that would have suited an anchorite. He seldom went out, ate nothing but salt fish, fruit, and whole-meal bread; he had several women in tow, but their company bored him. His only real pleasure (and one wondered how he existed before its advent) was the video player which he had going from morning till night, drawing upon a library of tapes that embraced most of the movies ever shot, from the early days of Hollywood classics to pornographic encounters filmed in back rooms of Soho with hand-held cameras last week. But every evening, at eight o'clock on the dot, the dross of the moving picture industry was swept aside for what the Man held to be the ultimate artistic, spiritual, and emotional feast ever created, beside which the Complete Works of Shakespeare, Michelangelo's Sistine Chapel murals, Beethoven's nine symphonies and five piano concertos, plus the entire output of Disney, were as nothing.

At eight o'clock on every day of his life (and nothing but World War III or the Second Coming would have prevented it) the Man watched *The Sound of Music,* starring Ms. Julie Andrews and Mr. Christopher Plummer, right through, credits and all.

On this particular evening, he was joining in—as usual—with the aria "My Favorite Things" when the intercom announced the arrival of Weasel Jilkes, who, because he knew his boss's routine and would never dare to interrupt the other's pleasure frivolously, must be calling upon a matter of some moment: not news of WW3, perhaps, nor yet the Second Coming, but something of a similar calibre. With this thought in his mind, the Man reluctantly pressed the pause button that stayed Ms. Andrews in a perpetual middle C, and activated the button that allowed his henchman to enter the armoured precinct.

"Well?" he demanded.

"Boss, the boys found O'Leary and the toff, both," was the other's triumphant news.

"Where?" The Man's delight, inwardly intense, did not manifest itself visibly to any degree; but there was a glint in his cold eyes such as one might see in a rattlesnake when, after

having watched some small, furry creature perish in agony
from its venom, it prepares to eat it whole.

"The boys have been patrolling St. James's and clubland,
like what you said, boss," said Weasel. "About an hour ago,
they sees O'Leary, the toff, and a young bird in a green Aston
Martin, and it's the bird who's driving. Next fing they know,
the Aston's pulled up outside the Ritz and the free of 'em gets
out. A flunkey from the hotel drives the car away to park it, the
bird says goodbye to the two geezers and goes in. And O'Leary
and the toff breeze off down Piccadilly."

"And the boys tail 'em, of course," said the Man.

Weasel writhed uncomfortably. "You're going to hate this,
boss," he said. "The boys lose 'em in the crowds—but!"—he
stabbed a finger to heighten the effect of his pay-off line—
"they suss out the bird wiv the Aston, and she's staying at the
Ritz."

"Put a tail on her," ordered the Man. "Day and night. As
soon as O'Leary shows again, day or night, someone move in
and rub him out—got that?"

"Trust me, boss," was the response. "I'll deal with that Irish
bastard myself."

"You do just that," gritted the Man. "And now you can get
the hell outa here." He stabbed the pause button.

"One thing's puzzling me, boss," said Weasel from the door.
"What happened to Darkie? It's like he was wiped off the face
of the earf!"

"Shut up and get out!" bleated the Man in his near-falsetto,
pointing to the image of Ms. Andrews resuming the modest
catalogue of her simple pleasures. "Ain't you got no feelings?"

Rosalind Purvis and Hannah McCracken were enjoying
more robust entertainment in their charming bijou *cottage
orné* in Kew: a TV presentation of *Lysistrata* by Aristophanes
in a new English translation. At the natural break, Hannah
went out to boil the kettle and wet the instant coffee that was
already measured out in their own individual mugs.

"A very funny thing when you were at the shops on Saturday morning, Roz," she called from the kitchen. "A couple of Americans were photographing the front of the cottage—or so I thought. But guess what . . ."

"What?"

"They were actually taking pictures of our two bottles of milk that had just been delivered on the doorstep. What do you think of that? Just as if they were heirlooms, or something."

"They don't have fresh milk delivered on the step in America any more," said Rosalind.

"That's what this nice couple said," responded Hannah, coming in with the coffee tray. "They got quite nostalgic about it."

"The French don't have it any more, either. Common Market regulations, I expect. We'll soon be the only country left in the world to have fresh cows' milk for our breakfast cornflakes."

They fell silent. Aristophanes aside, they had been silent with each other most of the evening; a constraint had fallen upon them ever since supper-time when the topic of their forthcoming holiday together (in Greece) had arisen. It had seemed to Hannah then that her friend appeared less enthusiastic than she might, considering that they were going the following Saturday, and in her habitual straightforward way she had said as much; Rosalind, in her habitual arcane manner, had denied any such thing. This had stung the former into a remark which, far from pouring oil on slightly troubled waters, was more like trying to put out a fire by throwing on petrol.

"Before we go off to Greece, it's to be hoped that you blow the whistle on that Major Arbuthnot character—or you're likely to find yourself out of a job when you come back."

Rosalind had simply not risen to the goad, but had relapsed into silence that only the small talk about the milk bottles had patched up—to a degree. And Hannah was now angry that her pacification attempt had fallen rather flat. When *Lysistrata* was resumed, she exhaled noisily through her nose and exclaimed, "You're not really trying to kid me that you're enjoying this pretentious crap, are you?"

"I think it's rather good," replied Rosalind mildly.

"Piffle!"

"But then again," said Rosalind, "as a former classical scholar, you probably prefer to hear it in the original—and look down your nose at semi-illiterates like me."

And this, for gentle-mannered Rosalind Purvis, was well below par for the course in her dealings with fiery Hannah McCracken!

For answer, Hannah went over to the TV and switched it off.

"I'm sorry," she said, "that my simple and unselfish regard for your well-being should call down on my head your biting sarcasm."

Rosalind sighed wearily. "Han, it's getting late," she said, "and we're both tired. Let's not fall out. I accept that your remark was well intended—but it was quite unnecessary.

"You see, I covered my stupidity by paying two thousand pounds into the Walbrook Trust's funds—so if anyone suffers from Major Arbuthnot's activities in this case, it will be me."

Her friend stared at her, open-mouthed with astonishment.

Presently she found her voice and said, "Are you telling me, Rosalind Purvis, that you dipped your hand in your own pocket to—to cover up for a personable crook?"

"Oh, don't be ridiculous, Han, it's not like that! I only—"

"In addition to throwing your money away, then—did you also go to the police?"

"Well, no, not yet. I—"

"I thought not!" cried Hannah. "I've been suspicious of your motives all along!" She pointed the accusing finger at the other. "You're stuck on that fellow! You met him twice for about five minutes and you're as besotted as a schoolgirl!"

Rosalind leapt to her feet, mild eyes blazing.

"That is not only ridiculous," she shouted, "but it's also bloody rude!"

They were all set for a bumpy night in the *cottage orné* at Kew.

Discounting, in O'Leary's case, the manifest advantages of having Myfanwy more or less on call, the Whitehaven Hotel in the Strand, while not to be compared with its neighbour the Savoy, provided them with a suite of two single rooms, with a sitting-room and integral bathroom—all quite cheaply. They also had a private telephone.

It was well past midnight when the phone rang in the living-room. Bunbury, who was wide awake, cheated on his companion and lay for a while in the hope that the other would respond and answer it. There being no action from the next room, he presently hauled himself out and did the honours—thinking at the time that the caller, whoever it was, possessed an admirable persistence to have gone on ringing for so long.

"Hello!"

"Listen—it's me. . . ."

"Mrs. Sawtry?"

"Yes. Listen. Something terrible's happened. You've got to come to the Ritz! Now! Right away!"

"But—"

"Right away—or we're all in trouble! I'll be waiting near the side entrance on Arlington Street. Hurry!"

The line went dead.

"What's up, Horse?" O'Leary was standing beside him, presumably having also played possum and waited for the other to answer the call.

Bunbury told him.

"Let's go!" said O'Leary. "That's a lady, if I ever saw one, who doesn't waste time by talking hot air. Fixed as we are, we're hers to command any time she blows the whistle.

"Come on!"

She was waiting for them—a dark shadow by the august wall of the great hotel—when they piled out of their late-night cab across the street. She was still wearing evening dress, with a lacy shawl that covered her head and trailed across her back and shoulders—nun-like.

"It's round the corner here," she said in a strained whisper that told of nerves bared and suffering.

It was her Aston Martin, neatly parked in a quiet street where it would presumably be saved from the tender ministrations of traffic wardens till morning. There was someone sitting in the driver's seat, and the driver's window was open. Drawing closer, the two men recognised the occupant with the help of the street lamp nearby.

"Mr. Colenso," said Bunbury.

"The *late* Mr. Colenso," Desirée corrected him in a tight voice.

"Gawd! He's as dead as mutton!" exclaimed O'Leary, who had put his head and shoulders through the window into the car. "You made a good, clean job of it, Mrs. Sawtry, I'll give you your due."

"Only—I didn't kill him!" she cried, touching a note of high hysteria.

O'Leary looked about them: there was no one in sight, and no sound. "Quickly, Mrs. Sawtry," he said, "what happened? Grab a hold on yourself and tell us exactly what took place."

"We went out to a night-club," she began, and she had her nerves in tight control now. "Not at his suggestion, the rat, but at George's, who thought I needed taking out of myself—the old fool!

"Zach was at his most repulsive. When he wasn't pawing me, he was trying to make time with the cigarette girl, the hat-check girl—anything that was around and available. I managed to get him out around midnight and he drove back. Outside the hotel, would you believe, he tried to get the dress off me right there in the car?—but I fought him off and bolted, leaving him to park.

"I hadn't barely got upstairs before I found I was missing one of my diamond earrings that George gave me only yesterday, so I came back down to see if I'd dropped it somewhere in the struggle.

"The Aston was parked right here where he'd put it. And he —he was like you see him!"

O'Leary was examining the body. Nudging his accomplice, he pointed to a thin trickle of blood that had emerged from the dead man's ear nearest the door. Also to a discreet splash of blood on the left breast of the dress shirt.

"There's a tiny hole here," he murmured, fingering the linen shirt. "No bigger than you'd make with a knitting needle. Someone stabbed him there to the heart. Then, to make sure, poked into his brain through the ear."

"Nasty," said Bunbury.

"Ain't it just?"

"You've got to get rid of him for me!" cried Desirée. "Like you promised. I didn't kill him (and believe me, I'd be rejoicing if I had), but I'm not taking the rap for some other dame he no doubt cheated on." She faced them squarely, all her nervousness gone: now she was all virago. "The key's in the car ignition. Get moving! Ring me in the morning to tell me everything's fixed okay.

"But not before eleven!"

She was already half-way back to the hotel when she called out the final directive.

The two accomplices looked in at the dead man, and then at each other.

" 'Strewth! We're having to earn that five millions bucks!" declared O'Leary. "We're having to do that, all right!"

"If we ever *see* it!" retorted Bunbury.

Bunbury had the marginal consolation of driving the Aston Martin through the park, along Kensington Gore, and putting into the given-over space alongside the Albert Hall. They then had to repeat the distasteful chore of handling the corpse: lifting it out of the back seat, arranging the limp arms over their own shoulders, and staggering with it across the road. No one saw them, and only one vehicle passed by in the time it took to mount the lower steps of the monument and elbow their way through a parting in the plastic sheeting.

"Thank God the moon's up," said O'Leary, "we wouldn't be able to risk a torch—even if we had one."

"Where do we put him? That's the question," said Bunbury.

They were standing on the top level of the monument, directly before Prince Albert's plinth: the bronze representation was staring down at them with discernible disfavour.

O'Leary tapped the pavement with his foot.

"Right here, Horse," he said. "Under this flagstone. Right under His Royal Highness's nose."

"It's one hell of a big flagstone!" breathed Bunbury. "Take ten men to lift it."

"We don't have ten men," retorted O'Leary, stripping off his coat and rolling up his sleeves. "So we'll have to make do with just the two of us, working two-and-two, in five shifts."

There were, of course, spades, shovels, pickaxes on the site, together with crowbars, ropes, pulleys, and so forth. Jamming a couple of stout crowbars into one end of the long flagstone plumb in the centre of the pavement, the two of them essayed to prise the block of granite out of its seating.

Minutes later, they downed tools and took off their shirts, which were wringing wet with sweat.

"Gosh, it's hot in here under that damned sheeting!" complained Bunbury. "Do you think we'll ever make it, Tom?"

"Concentrate on that five million smackers," gritted the other, "and keep bearing down on that crowbar."

Some time later—to the unhappy participants, it seemed like an aeon later—the end of the flagstone discernibly yielded to their efforts.

"We've got it on the move!" cried O'Leary. And he jammed the end of his crowbar into a gap that had appeared between their block and the one next door.

Ten minutes later, by the ancient method of leverage, not unconnected with dogged muscle power, they had the flagstone slid aside to disclose what lay underneath.

What lay immediately underneath was hard-packed rubble bound together with good mid-Victorian cement, upon which the flagstones had rested for well over a hundred years!

"We're making no impression!" complained Bunbury. "No blooming impression at all!"

There was not room for the two of them in the slight declivity left by the moving of the flagstone. The Englishman was standing in there, hacking away at the unyielding mass of cemented rubble with a pickaxe, and had so far removed enough to fill, say, a large breakfast cup. Stripped to the waist at first, he had now parted with his trousers for the sake of further coolness and was working in Y-front underpants, shoes, and socks, with a handkerchief tied round his brow as a sweat-rag.

"I'll take over for a while," said the Irishman and, suiting the action to the word, took his place in the declivity, swung his pickaxe—and cursed aloud when the shock of impact jarred his whole frame from wrists to heel-bones.

He rested on his pickaxe for a while. "Of course, we don't have to dig down very far."

"What a pity," said Bunbury with heavy irony. "Only a *little* hole? '. . . not so deep as a well, nor so wide as a church-door'?"

"That's right," said O'Leary. "Just enough so's we can lay the flagstone back down without squashing him."

"Please!" The other grimaced.

O'Leary re-addressed himself to his labours. After a while he brightened slightly. "Look, look," he said. "I've found the technique. Instead of banging away with brute force and bloody ignorance, one simply chips lightly—so—and persuades quite small pieces to detach themselves." Suiting the action to the words, he chipped—and a piece of material the size of a sparrow's egg broke free.

"By Jove, you're right!" exclaimed his companion. "Get out of the way and let me have a go."

The new technique worked. By half-past two in the morning they had removed enough rubble and cement to fill a fair-sized bucket.

And it was about then that—*it happened.* . . .

"Someone with a flashlight!" hissed Bunbury, who was "rest-

ing" at the time. "Over by the car-park! Looks as if he's in-
specting the Aston!"

"The cops!"

They peered out of a crack in the plastic sheeting. Clearly in
the street lighting, they could see a blue-uniformed figure
bending over the Aston Martin's suave rear end.

"He's taking the number!"

"Nothing to worry about. It's perfectly legal to leave a car
overnight in a private car-park. They'll trace it to Desirée, but
she'll cook up a convincing explanation."

"It only goes to show, though, how jolly careful you've got to
be. I mean—what if we'd been so stupid as to park it on a
double yellow line right in front of here!"

"He's going away now, thank God!"

"No he's not. . . ."

"He's crossing the road—he's coming here!"

"What do we do?"

"Make a bolt for it, across the gardens?"

"What about—him?" Pointing to the still form lying nearby.

"We can't bolt and carry him!"

"Leave him here? —Forget I said that!"

"I've got it!" said Bunbury, and leapt towards the corpse.

"What are you doing?" wailed O'Leary. "Have you gone out
of your mind entirely?"

"I'm stripping him—lend a hand!"

O'Leary obeyed, wrenching the trousers and underpants
from off the corpse. "I think I know what you're about," he
gritted, "but it'll never work—not in a month of Sundays."

"It's the only chance we have," responded Bunbury. "Remember the old saw about hiding a tree in a forest." He pulled
the dress shirt over the corpse's head, rendering it naked.
"Come on—up with him."

Together they manhandled the naked corpse over to the
plinth of the *America* group. Bunbury leapt up and, seizing
the defunct Colenso under the armpits, lifted the dead weight
up amongst the gesticulating statuary, with O'Leary shoving
on the legs.

It was then that Bunbury was struck by the fundamental fallacy of his idea. . . .

"These figures are all twice life-size and more!" he wailed. "He's out of proportion!"

"Put him up in *America*'s arms!" responded O'Leary. "He'll pass for a child in the dark!"

One near-superhuman lift—and Zachary Colenso, jailbird, womanizer, and heaven knows what else, was lying in the very Victorian arms of the marble Indian squaw, and nuzzled against her uncovered bosom.

"Here come his clothes!" said O'Leary, throwing them up. "And ours! Spread 'em out on the base, below eye-level."

Bunbury vaulted down and rejoined his companion. A glance over the shoulder, and the loom of the policeman's torch could be seen approaching up the long flight of steps.

"What about us?"

"Up—*there!*"

"There" was the continuous frieze of sculpted figures in high relief—all life-sized, all representing the great minds of world history up to mid-Victoriana.

"We'll never get away with it!" breathed O'Leary.

"Better than an even chance if we keep as still as statues," replied Bunbury. "Find yourself a place amongst the ancient Greeks and such chaps!"

They parted company. Racing—now barefoot and entirely naked—round the plinth to the rear, Bunbury saw a group of figures who looked to be Egyptian, or they might have been Assyrian—in any event they were all undressed, or close to it. Pulling himself up, he seized one of them round the shoulders and engaged him in conversation, his bare back and buttocks turned to anyone who might chance to look up.

Police Constable Hewitt Davis was coming to the end of his beat, and glad of it. Next there was the long walk down the right-hand, western side of Exhibition Road; a check of the Imperial College, Science Museum, Geological Museum—

then meet up with the sergeant at the corner of Cromwell Road. Report on anything doing—and off back home to bed.

Meanwhile, this convenient cover over the old Albert Memorial was a super place for a quiet drag. . . .

He took a match to light his cigarette—and was half tempted to strike it on the bare arse of the statue up there in the shadows. Very rude, those Victorians, despite all their sermonizing. Or perhaps because of it. He took a deep pull of his cigarette and exhaled the smoke.

That Aston Martin over in the car-park—some motor car, that. And a helluva place to leave it—right out in the open for anyone to nick, or vandalize. Some folks have got more money than sense. What was the time? Quarter to three. Just in time to do the Exhibition Road. Better be off. The break and a quick drag was very nice.

He stubbed out his cigarette on the ledge of the frieze, among the carved stone feet up there.

"Good night, gents," he said to the statuary. "Thanks for the hospitality."

He had reached the southern end of the monument and was about to duck under the plastic sheeting when something like a strangled cry coming from behind him caused him to pause —and listen.

Could be a cat, or even an urban fox. More foxes scavenging in the London parks than you'd find up in the shires.

P.C. Davis straightened his helmet and set off down the steps with a steady tread.

"Was that you who called out?" demanded O'Leary.

"Yes," answered Bunbury. "The cop only came in here for a sneaky ciggie. He half stubbed it out on the plinth, and the first time I moved I put my foot on the damned thing!"

"We were luckier than we deserve," said O'Leary, philosophizing as he picked away at the concrete and rubble. "The blighter never came near me."

Bunbury scooped up a double handful of the stuff that they

had taken out of the grave-to-be: it seemed a very large proportion of their night's work so far.

"Do you suppose we'll have it finished by daylight?" he asked.

"I doubt it," was the rejoinder. "But we'd better have him safely under the slab before those three clowns of ours turn up at nine o'clock!"

Dawn broke early. The first sleepy-eyed commuters were wending their way to work while the grave was still too shallow to take a cut-out figure in thick cardboard, let alone a three-dimensional man. Happily, once they had removed the first few intractable inches, the going became easier, the rock-like cement not so much in evidence, and a certain amount of earth was mixed in with the rubble. The two diggers blessed the slackness of the long-dead Victorian navvies—and the careless overseeing of their foreman—for the respite.

At eight thirty-five exactly, they threw aside pickaxe and shovel, satisfied that they had a grave fit for a man. And so it proved: the last remains of Zachary Colenso, laid in the declivity with his clothes draped over the top of the corpse, permitted the flagstone to be replaced with ease.

They stood back and surveyed their handiwork. It was as if the block of stone had never been moved, that the man named Zachary Colenso (now fated to remain for ever beneath the disapproving glance of Prince Albert) had never been.

The "three clowns" arrived a quarter of an hour late, having already partaken of fermented grain in an alehouse that opened early for the benefit of workers in Smithfield meat market. Recalling that he had the all-important luncheon engagement with the unfrocked member of Parliament turned launderer, O'Leary summoned a cab to take him back to the hotel for a bath and a change, and Bunbury went with him. Dickie, Norman, and Hugo watched their employers' departure, then each went to a quiet part of the monument to sleep off his early morning's excesses.

At eleven o'clock, as ordered, Bunbury put through a call to

Mrs. George G. Sawtry at the Ritz. Desirée, still in bed, took the call.

"It's done," was his cryptic message.

"I never felt so good in my life!" she replied—a response which, in what he regarded as its sheer callousness, offended his sensibilities.

She replaced the receiver, cynically aware that her reaction had displeased him. "All right for you, Mr. Swell-guy, whatever you call yourself," she soliloquized. "You could never imagine the kind of rat who'd marry a hired waitress in his cocktail lounge and then send her down there to work—topless, as usual—on her wedding night, while he made time upstairs with another dame."

To her surprise, she found that she was in tears.

The disciplines of prison having sloughed from the Man, he now had no difficulty in sleeping through till noon; indeed he steadfastly refused to do business before that hour once the late-rising habit had been restored. Not till then, therefore, on that particular day, did Weasel Jilkes announce his arrival in the familiar manner and gain admittance.

He found his employer floating in the swimming pool on his back, vastly convex in the anterior parts and like a basking whale.

"Boss—I got him!" announced the newcomer jubilantly. "I got that Irish bastard for you!"

The Man, not often given to the visual expression of any sort of emotion, palpably beamed to hear this news; climbed out of the pool and, whilst permitting his henchman to dry him down with a Turkish bath towel, demanded to know the details.

"Howja fix him?" he demanded. "Don't tell me you gunned him down from some top window, or ran him over maybe, or spiked his drink wiv prussic. None of these is safe and sure. I know more guys who wuz filled with lead at a hunnerd yards and is still collecting their old age pensions."

"I fixed him with—the hat-pin," said the other with some coyness.

"The hat-pin!" The nearest to a smile that had ever enhanced the Man's unaccommodating features burst forth on this one occasion. "The hat-pin—I might've guessed! My, Weasel, I remember fine as how you wuz always quick and nifty with the pin. But tell me how—and when. . . ."

"Boss, after the boys had fingered the bird with the Aston," said Weasel, "me and the boys kept a round-the-clock watch on the Ritz. At eight last night, one of 'em gets on the blower to me and sez that O'Leary and the bird is off to some night spot, all togged up to the nines, in the Aston.

"Well, the rest is easy. I wait around till they come back. The bird, she gets shirty 'cos maybe he wants to play around a little. She jumps out. He drives the Aston round the corner and parks it. I stroll up, lean in the window, and ask him for a light.

"And then—zip!—zip! He's as dead as a jellied eel."

"Lovely!" The Man let the word roll off his tongue like liquid velvet. "Really lovely."

Weasel Jilkes, preening himself at this highly uncustomary praise, presumed upon his greatly inferior position to pose a question to his employer. Let it be said that he had been a member of the latter's entourage for rather less time than most, having joined only a few months before the Man was sent up to serve his recent term at the Scrubs. By rumour, word of mouth (never very well substantiated), and direct observance of his employer's reactions, he had formed a very marked impression about the boss's relationship with the man he himself had come to refer to as "that Irish Bastard."

"Boss," he said in as ingenuous a tone as he could muster, "how come you wuz always so set against O'Leary? Right from the fust I knew you, it wuz always your ambition—to wipe him out." Greatly daring, he added, "What did O'Leary ever do to you?"

"What did he do to me?" The thin voice fluted high to a note of fury, and Weasel thought he had gone too far.

"I'll tell you what the bastard did to me! . . ."

THE GREAT WORMWOOD SCRUBS CON.
An Intermezzo

Thomas Aquinas O'Leary, after he left the Guards' Division under a cloud of disgrace (but greatly missed by all ranks from the humblest guardsman to his colonel), did not so much *drift* into the life of crime as take his rightful place as a leading exponent—a consultant specialist, one might be tempted to say—in that most rarefied of felonious activities: high-class confidence trickery.

O'Leary's pre-eminence in his chosen field stemmed from his philosophy that People—the great Public—the potential "marks" of this world—have a built-in weakness as regards officialdom, in that they always respond *positively* to officialdom's stimuli, whether it be a Tax Demand, a Summons to appear in Court, or even a bland letter from some petty official advising them that, owing to a regrettable error, they are due for a refund of a derisory sum of money. The People will accept all these stimuli without question.

So much for the homespun philosophy. Allied to this instinctive know-how, O'Leary had also made himself, through practice, a printer and typographer of considerable skill, and a master of pastiche in the forging of official communications.

That, then, was the whole bedrock upon which his career as an ace con man was founded.

In the rarefied part of the underworld in which he moved, O'Leary the ex–Guards officer never rubbed shoulders with the likes of the Man, whose activities with drugs, extortion, protection, and prostitution were as alien and distasteful to him as they would have been to any of his former messmates at Chelsea Barracks. He was, nevertheless, well aware that the Man was absolute ruler of his own seedy enclave, and that he could buy or sell him. This greatly rankled with O'Leary, who had an artist's pride in his skills, and contempt for the other's grubby activities; accordingly, he planned to set matters right by pulling a massive confidence trick on the contemptible

Cuthbert Judd, alias the Man. And this is how he pulled it off. . . .

TO: PRISON DEPARTMENT
The Governor   89 Eccleston Square,
Her Majesty's Prison   London, S.W.1
Wormwood Scrubs, W.12   Tel: (01) 828 9848
                                             Date as postmark

CONFIDENTIAL

Sir,

In conformity with Government Policy outlined in Confidential Clauses Nos. 1–6 of the White Paper on Disposal & Rebuilding (1985–1995 Programme), H.M. Prison Wormwood Scrubs will shortly be put up for sale by private auction under the terms already communicated to you, which, to recapitulate, call for a very minimum of publicity and—more important—public speculation.

The delicacy of the sale relates, as you know, to the peculiar condition by which the Crown Lease is held in perpetuity. Briefly, under a statute of King Charles II (which is deemed to have been a *lapsus calami,* but which cannot legally be revoked), the site and any buildings thereon are free in perpetuity of all restrictions as regards the sale of liquor, facilities for gambling, and—most regrettably—what was referred to in the 17th Century statute as "ye procurement of ladys of easie virtue."

This letter is to remind you of the necessity for confidentiality regarding the private sale, the Home Secretary being most concerned at the prospect of the site and buildings falling into the hands of improper persons who might make ill use of the 17th Century statute.

You are informed that the private auction will take place at the Braganza Hotel, Buckingham Palace Road, on the 5th of next month at 6 P.M. A purchase price adjacent to £2,000,000 has been indicated.

Yours faithfully,
  [Signed]
  Assistant Deputy Director-General
  of the Prison Service

The above document, the work of Tom O'Leary as typographer-printer and master of pastiche, did not in fact arrive on the desk of the governor of Wormwood Scrubs. One photostat copy of it was made and the original destroyed. The copy, suitably folded, refolded, crumpled, and stained with splashes of suitable beverages, found its way into the possession of the Man. It was said to have been obtained by a discharged Scrubs prisoner who, as a trusty, had been charged with the job of cleaning out the governor's office, in which capacity he had come across the department's letter, and had found the means to make a copy. The Man paid quite handsomely for the service and passed it to his lawyer, one Rube Silver of Hackney, for comment.

Rube attested that the document was genuine and that the *lapsus calami,* or slip of the pen, might well have happened in the slap-happy era of Charles II's loose-living Restoration. He advised his client to make a bid for the property in question on the grounds that such an acquisition amounted to the free right to provide booze, gambling, and birds right round the clock—and sucks boo to the law.

Not only this enticing prospect, but also the memory of the long and bitter months and years he had languished in the Scrubs, motivated the Man to put in a bid for the property. Accordingly, he commissioned Rube Silver to attend the private sale, but to fight shy of the indicated figure and bid no higher than £1,500,000. (It should be added that there was never any question of the Man's attending the auction, for he never actively participated in any of his criminal enterprises, even at the perimeters, but spent most of his life moving between his penthouse pad, his club, and sundry public houses.)

Through the same discreet means by which Silver was ad-

vised of the means to gain access to the private sale, he was
also informed that T. A. O'Leary, backed by a syndicate that
had agreed to provide the capital to develop the property into
what was described as a "Libido Complex," was the only other
punter known to be in the running. Hearing of this, the Man—
who heartily despised O'Leary as an unfrocked swell and an
amateur—dismissed the competition out of hand. Where
would a small-time con man like that Irish geezer raise a
million and a half upwards?

The Man's chagrin may be pictured when it was heard that
the Scrubs had been knocked down to O'Leary for the incon-
siderable sum of £1,250,000. Rube Silver had not been present
to put in a bid owing to a small accident he had suffered on the
way to the auction. Apart from a few superficial bruises, no
real harm had come to him, but the suggestion—delivered by
his masked assailants—that the removal of certain of his vital
appendages might follow his attendance at the sale persuaded
him to return to his little wife and neat little home in Hackney
Wick.

Several days passed, during which time the Man was unap-
proachable to any of his subordinates. He threw crockery and
broke glassware, mortally insulted at least two of his fellow
East End gang leaders over the phone, and set in train a bitter
three-cornered vendetta—so great was his fury at being
bested by "that Irish bastard."

Presently, however, the Man's mortification turned to tri-
umph—with the news that O'Leary had been deserted by his
backers, the proposed Libido Complex doomed to remain no
more than an architect's dream drawing, and the bank was
dunning him for the one and a quarter million they had advanced for the sale. Moreover, O'Leary was putting it about
that he was willing to "sell on" the property for a figure not
unadjacent to his purchase price—with the slight panic hint
that he might be persuaded to accept considerably less.

Like a cat playing with a wounded mouse, the Man was in no
great hurry to close in for the kill. Being assured by his inform-

ers that there was no other punter in the running, he let the
Irishman sweat it out for a couple of weeks—indeed, till he
learned that O'Leary's bank had foreclosed on him and had
applied to the court for a judgement. He then blandly offered
£950,000 for his old "college" and, knowing full well to what
desperate ends a man may be driven when the fat hits the fan,
was not one whit surprised when his offer was accepted with
alacrity.

He now "owned" Wormwood Scrubs, lock, stock, and barrel.
Oh, the joy! . . .

The joy of summoning the Roller, with one of his henchmen
tricked out in chauffeur's rig. The sheer delight of wearing his
new winter coat—the one with the astrakhan collar, topped off
with a curly-brimmed Homburg, with a diamond tie-pin at his
thick throat and stones of a like water shimmering on his
fingers and cuff-links. The ecstasy of alighting from the Roller
and, strutting up to the forbidding front gate with a Romeo y
Julieta stuck in the corner of his mouth, to hammer upon it for
admittance.

It took the Man a little while to convince the door warden of
his business, but after considerable argument the latter was
persuaded to telephone through to the governor's secretary
and deliver a garbled rendition of the newcomer's needs and
requirements.

The then governor of Wormwood Scrubs was a humane man
possessed of a sprightly sense of humor. Furthermore, like all
his confrères right down the line of the prison hierarchy, he
knew Cuthbert Judd, alias the Man, by name and reputation,
but had never had him reckoned as a prankster. More from
curiosity than anything, he decided to see the visitor and hear
from his own lips the outrageous assertion that he had hinted
at to the door warden.

And lo!—there he was. In his coat with the astrakhan collar,
still wearing his jaunty hat even before the august presence of
the governor, puffing expensive Havana cigar smoke into the
outraged face of the chief warder, who stood at his master's
elbow and disapproved of the entire adventure.

The good-natured governor heard the Man out; perused the certainly genuine-seeming legal document that purported to deliver the site of Wormwood Scrubs, together with the buildings thereon, the tenements and messuages and so forth, for the sum of £950,000 from the former owner Thomas Aquinas O'Leary, Captain, Irish Guards (Retd.).

It was then, satisfied that he had made his point, that the Man's cup ran over, and he had the greatest pleasure in demanding the keys from the governor and ordering him—together with his staff and inmates—off the premises. *His* premises.

At that the governor collapsed in a paroxysm of mirth, in which he was joined by his chief. So incensed was the Man by this display of what he took to be contempt that—though far from being a violent person—he assaulted both men with the silver-knobbed cane that he carried, sustaining such injuries upon their persons that he was later charged with Grievous Bodily Harm and sentenced in the Old Bailey to twelve months' imprisonment. And, by a bitter irony, he was condemned to serve this time at his old "college."

Nine hundred and fifty thousand pounds to the bad, twelve months less remission for good conduct in the Scrubs—despite that, the Man's torment was not yet done. When he came out, it was to endure a tremendous loss of face among his fellow leaders of the London underworld, for though the unofficial trade unionism that binds together the tsars of organized crime prevented the big shots from allowing details of the Man's disgrace to percolate downwards to the rank and file of the criminal fraternity for fear of causing general dissatisfaction with the leadership, they had no qualms about making the Man's personal life a hell on earth. He was ostracized from the tightly knit community of his peers: no ringside seats at the big fights for "Juddie" (the affectionate nickname by which Cuthbert Judd had once been addressed by his intimates), nor similar perks in the centre court at Wimbledon; he was never seen at gangland weddings, funerals, bar mitzvahs, Christmas parties; when "Cut-throat" Morrie Spender's boy was called to the Bar, there was no invitation to his celebration cocktail party at the Dorchester. In short, the Man was OUT. The tremendous social advantages that accrue from sitting on the top of the crime heap in London were denied him for so long as he remained under the stigma of having been bested by an upstart con artist who was no more than a talented amateur, and a Mick to boot.

Driven from the limelight, the Man retreated into a voluntary purdah that was bounded more and more by the four walls of his penthouse pad, a dark corner of his club, ditto a few public houses, and the interior of his silver Rolls-Royce; an existence adumbrated by the constant threat of prison sentences brought upon himself by his continued master-minding of criminal activities by his gang; a poor way of life sweetened only by *The Sound of Music* nightly at eight.

But now—as he told Weasel Jilkes when the latter reported the (wrongfully assumed) death of T. A. O'Leary, the man who had ruined him both professionally and socially—the debt was now paid, an eye had been taken for an eye, a tooth for a tooth.

The Man was vindicated before his peers, and could walk tall again.

EIGHT

There was still a policeman on guard outside the merchant bank in Leadenhall Street, though the discreet notice of closure had been removed. The arm of the law, bored and shirt-sleeved in the baking heat of the man-made city canyon, watched with only mild interest when a Rover car drew up on the forbidden double yellow line almost abreast of him. This vehicle—black, not quite new but beautifully kept, chauffeur-driven, and exuding officialdom—was of the sort much favoured by higher civil servants of all branches: a student of Whitehall mores might deduce that the well-maintained vintage Rover is the car most esteemed by the Home Office in particular.

The chauffeur darted out smartly and opened the passenger door, from which alighted a tall, grey-haired, and bearded man in a City suit and bowler hat, bearing the ubiquitous brief-case and rolled umbrella. He gave an order to the other that the policeman did not quite pick up, but he distinctly heard the chauffeur reply to the bearded man with a respectful "Yes, Sir Hubert."

Sir Hubert whoever mounted the steps with an athletic spring to his gait and regarded the attendant constable with shrewd appraisal.

"I am expected, Officer," he announced.

"Yessir!" replied the policeman, saluting. He rang the bell, which presently caused the door to be opened by a somewhat harassed-looking individual in shirt-sleeves, with a green eye-shade, a pencil tucked behind an ear, and a whole battery of the same arraigned in the top pocket of his vest.

"Sir Hubert Garstad?" he enquired. "They telephoned to

tell me you were on your way. Please follow me, sir. Everything's in a terrible mess. The Fraud Squad were here. Turned everything out—all the cupboards and drawers, filing cabinets —everything. What they didn't take away with them they left all over the place." He glanced anxiously at his companion and tried to read his expression in the gloomy hallway, full of shadows now that the door was closed behind them. "I suppose you'll be adding to the mess, sir—no offence intended."

Garstad smiled. "No, I leave that kind of thing to the fraud boys. My task is to winnow through what remains after the onslaught and pick up unconsidered trifles they might have missed. You'll scarcely notice my passing."

"I'm glad to hear that, Sir Hubert," replied the other. "You should see the job I've got downstairs. Piles of boxes and folders thrown everywhere—and all got to be sorted out, indexed, and packed off to the Board of Trade with the rest. This way, sir. Mind your step."

The narrow corridor beyond the hallway was piled ceiling-high each side with box files and japanned tin trunks, some of them opened and spilling their contents.

"You'll be wanting the boss's office, sir," said Garstad's guide.

"That's right," replied the other. "You can leave me there to pry around. When I've finished, I'll telephone for my car and let myself out."

"Here we are, sir." The man in the eye-shade opened a door into a panelled room furnished with a handsome eighteenth-century knee-hole desk and a swing chair, fitted bookcases, a leather couch. A grave-faced portrait of a man in a bag-wig hung above a marble fireplace.

Laying aside his hat, umbrella, and brief-case, Garstad sat down in the swing chair and ruefully eyed the desk. The drawers were all part-open, revealing jumbles of paper within.

"You'll not find much that hasn't been gone through half a dozen times over, sir," said his companion.

"You'd be surprised at some of the things I turn up," said Garstad.

"They say the boss was a real gentleman. Married, with kids.

Everything to live for. Strange, what makes folks go off the rails like he did."

"Mmmm, I knew him well," mused Garstad.

"It's the family I feel sorry for, sir. Still, I expect he left them well provided for."

"Save for the small matter of his reputation."

"Beg pardon, sir?"

"Oh, nothing. Well, I won't keep you any longer, Mr.—er—"

"Forbrush, sir. Board of Trade records. I'm like the chap who follows after the Lord Mayor's Parade with a bucket and shovel."

"Well, thank you, Mr. Forbrush."

"Good hunting, Sir Hubert."

Alone, the grey-bearded man relaxed in the seat for a minute or so and looked about him. Next, running his fingers along the edge of the desk, under the overhang, he presently came upon a piece of moulding which, upon a slight pressure, pivoted aside to reveal to his probing fingertips a small orifice into which he was able to fit a tiny key that hung on a thin chain about his neck. A turn of the key released a catch that permitted him to remove an elaborately carved panel in the knee-hole. Reaching under, he took from the hidden recess three buckram-bound quarto volumes which he laid on the tooled leather desk-top before him, and opened the uppermost.

"Now, let's see what you've been up to, Walter old chap," he murmured aloud, addressing himself to the descriptive notes and the columns of figures—their totals carried forward from every page—which made up the body of the contents.

The ormolu shepherdess clock on the chimney-piece thinly tinkled the midday hour by the time he had perused the first volume and pushed it to one side.

Again he commented quietly to himself, "Went in a bit over your head, I'd say, Walter. No wonder everything came apart in your fingers, poor chap."

The three books were composed in diary form, each representing two years, and every page relating to one week, with entries set out one above the other. He gave each page a cursory glance, focusing on a more protracted attention to those entries which featured a familiar name, or a particularly large sum of money. In this manner, he gutted the general content of all three volumes, till, reaching the final written-upon pages of the third, he came to items that had been entered in the current week and the week preceding.

The very last item . . . this:

> 29th Monday: *Most Immediate.* Launder via Paris, Marrakesh, Zurich. Calling tomorrow at 9:30 A.M. The O'Leary Connection. (Phone 992-6754)
> *Amount involved* (drawn on a Bank of Madison & Wall Street cheque). . . . .
> $5,000,000

The bearded man sat back and emitted a long, soft whistle. "Well, well, it's a small world," he observed. "Who would have believed it?"

He paid not the slightest attention to the remainder of the desk's contents, nor did he search the rest of the room; with the discovery of the three volumes, his task was finished. Placing them carefully in his brief-case, he picked up hat and umbrella and made his departure, not did he telephone for his car as he had indicated to the functionary named Forbrush.

The constable on the door sprang to attention and saluted when the grey-bearded man went out and down the steps, acknowledging the tribute by raising his bowler. Crossing the busy road, he turned up the first intersection and then again at the next. Three blocks further on, he descended into an underground lavatory, locked himself in a cubicle, and, removing the grey wig he wore, together with the false beard and moustache, placed them in the brief-case along with the volumes. Lastly, he peeled off the almost undetectable skin of flesh-coloured latex which, sprayed on his hands to form a glove, had ensured that he had left no trace of his passing through the merchant bank.

Ten minutes later, he let himself out of the cubicle and set off to find the nearest telephone kiosk.

"So where is he, then? Three times I rang his room. The chambermaid went in there and found his bed hadn't been slept in. So what happened to the guy? This is London, England—not someplace in the Middle East. Guys don't get kidnapped on every street corner here like they was nickels and dimes lying around for the taking."

George G. Sawtry so addressed his lady at cocktail time.

Desirée said, "Maybe he went for a walk."

"First making his bed, maybe?" countered he with only the lightest touch of sarcasm.

She shrugged. "I'm not his keeper," she said. "You want to play private eye, go right ahead."

He glanced at her narrowly: for a basically amiable person, Sawtry could produce a very narrow look.

"Did you two kids have a fight last night?" he asked.

"About what?" she countered.

"Well—at a guess—who should pick up the tab at the night-club," he said. "I told you to do the honours, but a straight up-and-down regular feller like young Zach would resent having to accept money from a woman. Uh, what did you say, hon?"

"Oh, it was nothing," responded Desirée, smiling, despite herself, into her Martini. "Nothing at all."

"Well, I'm going to put Tex and the boys onto looking around for him," declared Sawtry. "And if he ain't turned up by, say, three o'clock, I'm going to report him to the police as a missing person. Desirée, I value that cousin of yours, I really do."

With that, the multimillionaire signalled a passing bellboy and made his wants known, contingent upon which Tex Manacle was summoned and given his orders: the hotel, the St. James's area, and the bars and public houses within it were to be searched for the missing paragon. No stone to be left unturned, and a report by word of mouth brought back by three o'clock at the latest.

Metaphorically buckling a phantom gun-belt about his paunchy waist, Tex strode forth to collect the posse and ride out to do Eagle-eye's bidding.

"Then why no report in the midday edition?"

The scene in the Man's penthouse pad paralleled that between George G. Sawtry and his lady in many respects: for the former, read the Man; for the latter, Weasel Jilkes; and the burden of the former's lament was the same in both cases: what had happened to the one known by Sawtry as Zachary Colenso and to the Man (in pardonable error) as T. A. O'Leary?

"It ain't every day that a stiff turns up in a car outside the Ritz," said the Man, rephrasing his argument; "why, then, ain't it splashed all over the front page of the second edition? That's what I wanna know!"

Weasel searched for a penetrating answer. "Mebbe he was crowded out by the news of the transport strike?" he suggested penetratingly.

"It's dead guys, not strikes, that sell papers!" piped the Man, his voice rising ever more shrilly in his excitement. "If you'd done the job properly, the story would have been plastered everywhere and on the TV news.

"And what was the big story on the TV at midday?

"I'll tell you—the giant panda in the Moscow zoo gave birth to twins!"

He strode up and down the yielding Persian carpet that had once graced the harem of a khan, the scheming brain that had raised him from the gutter to the apex of the underworld's dung heap battling behind that imperious brow. Presently he stopped and pointed to Weasel Jilkes, who shrank away.

"You blew it!" declared the Man. "There ain't no other explanation what fits. Don't bluster at me, Weasel—you blew it! That hat-pin didn't do no more than scratch a rib or two and clean the wax outa his ear. The Irish bastard is alive and kicking!"

Another orgy of pacing up and down, and his massive intellect swept, like a hawk descending, upon a solution. Again he pointed at his cringing henchman and declaimed, "That bird —the one wiv the Aston Martin what's staying at the Ritz— she's the key!

"Latch on to her. Find out who she is, who she's with, every-thing about her. Follow her everywhere. Don't let her outa your sight. If she goes to the little girls' room, you be there waiting outside the door, and one of the boys watching from the street in case she hops outa the window.

"If anybody knows where O'Leary is, that bird does, and if we have to we'll lean on her till she sings like a canary.

"Off you go! Get fings moving in that direction!"

With no more ado, Weasel Jilkes went. And though it was still short of one o'clock in the afternoon, the Man diverged from his normally immutable habit and, in order to sooth his tangled nerve-ends, put on his video of *The Sound of Music.*

"How did you get on with the erring ex–member of Parlia-ment?"

Bunbury posed this question to his accomplice when they met up under the plastic awning of the monument in the early afternoon. "Not too well, I suppose, since the luncheon wasn't greatly protracted."

O'Leary pulled a long lip. "Furthermore," he said, "the swine claimed that he'd left his credit cards behind and I was landed with the tab. No, Horse old chap, he was a dead loss. Would you credit that a guy who, for all his faults, was once a junior minister of the Crown and very authoritatively tipped for a department should descend to out-welshing the cheapest of bucket-shops by asking 65 per cent—65, mark you!—to launder our cheque?"

"You didn't accept, of course?"

"To be honest, old son," replied O'Leary, "given that the offer had come from anyone else, I would have—working on the premise that 35 per cent of five million is better than no bread. But that wasn't the full extent of his knavery—the bas-tard demanded that I hand the cheque over to him, and not a penny piece would we receive till the damn thing was cleared in New York."

"But, surely," said Bunbury, "you gave me to understand that this was the procedure we must expect from anyone who handles the deal—like your friend of the merchant bank who shot himself."

"True enough," conceded O'Leary. "But would you put our cheque into the sticky fingers of a guy who would slip ten-pence tip into the lavatory attendant's plate—and sneak fifty out?"

"He never did that—*not* a former junior minister?"

"I saw him do it!"

"Mmm—I take your point."

They gazed gloomily across to where Dickie, Norman, and Hugo were leaning against the plinth of the *America* group and playing gin rummy. The preparations for raising and transporting the group finished, there remained only the sawing up of the figures to be accomplished—a feat that Norman D'Arcy of vaudeville fame had apportioned for himself just as soon as the stone-saw arrived, and it was expected at any hour. Meanwhile, there was gin rummy to while away the hot afternoon.

"Well, it's nearly over," said O'Leary. "To look on the bright side, we shall be shut of the Sawtrys tomorrow evening. There are rumours that the transport strike is crumbling. With any luck, we could be in Zurich by Friday, with a chance to talk that cheque into a numbered Swiss bank account before Sawtry realizes that he won't be getting the rest of the monument, and puts a stopper on our five million."

"Is the transportation fixed?" asked Bunbury.

"I rang the contractor," replied his partner. "The crates containing the goods will be loaded up and ready to move out to Heathrow by late afternoon tomorrow. I suggest that we contact the mark and put it to him that we all—his party included—leave for the airport in convoy from outside the Ritz at, say, six-thirty, in time for their eight o'clock flight to New York in the big chartered freighter."

"Good idea," endorsed the other. "Might as well send them off in style."

"You chaps," said Bunbury, addressing the "three clowns" joshingly, "had better gird up your loins for some real hard work just as soon as that saw arrives. You've got till this time tomorrow to cut up the statues, ready for them to be crated up and loaded."

There was no reply: the trio had fallen asleep over their cards.

Three o'clock had come and gone. Tex Manacle and his posse having come across neither hair nor hide of Zachary Colenso, the faithful major-domo-cum-bodyguard reported as much to his boss, who was taking a post-prandial nap in the hotel lounge in preparation for his tea. Desirée had departed upstairs for a lie-down—or so she claimed.

"You searched everywhere, Tex?" reiterated George G. Sawtry. "I would not press you so hard, old comrade, but I hold that boy in very high regard as the kind of surrogate son to whom it is my ambition one day to turn over the reins of that great covered wagon which is my ship of state—if I may be permitted the metaphor."

"Every pub, every bar, every street corner and whore-house, Eagle-eye," confirmed Tex. "We even called in at the local precinct and checked out that no one of his description was in the drunk-tank. There was not, nor had been."

Sawtry winced slightly. "In many regards it could be said that you exceeded the bounds of your search, Tex," he opined. "If he was not in one of the more select bars or public houses, one can only assume that some ill has befallen him. As I remarked earlier, though this is London, England, and the chances of his being kidnapped are slight, I am nevertheless determined to report his absence to the cops. See to that, willya, Tex?"

"Sure, Eagle-eye."

"Let's face it, with all my millions, I could be regarded as the kind of relation by marriage who would make a classic mark to any kidnapper."

"That's so, Eagle-eye."

"Then you communicate with the cops, Tex—and I'll go upstairs and bear the disquietening news to my lady wife."

Arriving in Desirée's bedroom, he found her lying there in a black chiffon negligee with an open and half-consumed box of chocolates on the bedside table at her elbow. She looked up from her glossy magazine, put down her lorgnette, and eyed him unenthusiastically as he entered.

"Honey," began Sawtry, assuming the kind of expression he felt suited to the occasion, "I'm sorry to tell you that Zach— that that fine young man—"

"He rang me just now," she interposed.

"He—*rang* you?"

"Sure. Last night, when he was parking my automobile, he met up with a buddy he had at the Oxford college, you know."

"Oxford—aaah." Sawtry's expression brightened.

"The friend—his name's Harry—suggested they both drive on down to the horse races. And that's where he rang me from —the horse races."

"The races! Well, that explains everything. Um—where's the races at, honeybun?"

"Where at?" Desirée looked disaccommodated, but not for long. "Why, at Stratford-upon-Avon," she said, this being the only place outside London that sprang readily to her lips.

"That's a great relief to me, hon," said Sawtry. "And to you, also, I don't doubt."

"Me? Oh, sure." Desirée picked up her magazine and her lorgnette.

Sawtry buttonholed Tex downstairs just as he came out of the phone booth from alerting the police to Colenso's disappearance. "The heat's off, Tex," he told his aide. "The boy's at the Stratford-upon-Avon races."

"Stratford-upon-Avon?" repeated the other and, pushing back his ten-gallon hat, he scratched his bald pate. "But, Eagle-eye, there ain't no race-track at Stratford-upon-Avon.

Brighton, they got a race-track, likewise Lansdown, Perth, Newton Abbot, Newmarket, and Newbury, to name but six." He fished in the hip pocket of his tight pants and brought out a folded newspaper, which he opened out at the back page devoted to the Sport of Kings. "Today is racing at Newmarket and at Newbury," he elaborated. "And I have a couple pounds on a hoss named Titty-Fallah, who is running in the two-thirty. Likewise, I have five of the best on another called Standfast, who the tipsters say will romp home first in the third race at Newbury.

"Nowhere have I ever heard tell of a race-track at Stratford-upon-Avon!"

Tex, whom his employer knew to be an inveterate gee-gee man, could not possibly be wrong in this assertion—a fact that caused Sawtry great unease.

"Then the phone call was a put-up job!" he cried. "The kidnappers not having yet secured that poor boy in a safe hideaway, they are doubtless not yet ready to tip off their hand, so they force Zach to give the phoney cover story to his cousin, to buy a little time!"

Tex nodded, perceiving the undoubted truth of the other's reasoning; by such mental agility had the other become a multimillionaire while he himself remained only a glorified cowpoke.

"So—what now, Eagle-eye?" he asked.

"So now you get back to the police again!" responded Sawtry. "But not a word to the little woman. I don't want her worried. And don't let her out of your sight, Tex. If the kidnappers really mean business, it's my little butterfly they'll snatch in the end—knowing, as they must, that I'd give every cent I have to prevent them from hurting one hair on her head.

"Get back onto the police again, Tex! Tell 'em to spare no effort, but track down the guys who're holding Zachary Colenso before they turn their attentions to my little woman.

"Thank Gawd we're going back home tomorrow. That guy Abey said he'd made all the arrangements and he'd be ringing me with the schedule. What happened to him?"

Still fussing, George G. Sawtry left his aide to fix matters with the Metropolitan police, while he went back up to his suite again, as much as anything to reassure himself that Desirée was still safe and sound.

A figure taking tea in a corner of the room covertly watched him over the rim of his cup. Dressed in white flannels, multicoloured blazer, and tie, with a straw boater parked nonchalantly on the seat opposite, he looked for all the world as if he had just come from Henley Royal Regatta; but anyone less likely to enter for such as the Diamond Sculls than the stunted and weedy Weasel Jilkes it would be hard to imagine.

O'Leary rang the mark within the hour. The latter sounded somewhat shrill when he answered the telephone, then greatly relieved to learn who it was, and even more so when he heard the arrangements for the departure to Heathrow.

"Sawtry sounds as hysterical as an old maid with her knickers in a twist," said O'Leary to his companion. "Must be having a male menopause. Anyhow, it's all fixed for tomorrow. What was that you said just now?"

Bunbury was lying on top of his single bed, stockinged feet propped up on the tailboard, a half-drunk cup of tea on his bedside table. He had been listening absently to O'Leary's phone call. "I was asking you, as paymaster, what was left of the working money we conned out of the Walbrook Trust."

"Speaking as paymaster," replied O'Leary, "there's over a grand left. We haven't had a bill from the Plantagenet yet."

"I wonder," said Bunbury, "if I could have five hundred on account?"

"Sure," said the other without hesitation. He took out his wallet, counted out a wad of twenties, and placed them on the table beside Bunbury's cup.

The latter glanced up at him, surprised. "Just like that?" he asked. "Don't you want to know what I want it for?"

O'Leary shrugged. "It's bound to be for something that's important to you," he said. "And likely to be no particular business of mine—or you'd have mentioned it."

"Tom, you're very trusting," said Bunbury. "I've decided that you must be a very nice guy."

The Irishman grinned. "Very popular with old ladies and dogs—some dogs," he said. "That's me. Speaking of trust"—again he went to his wallet—"it's your turn tomorrow to take care of the cheque. Better have it now, while we remember."

It had been tacitly agreed between them from the first that the precious cheque should never be left in their luggage, but always carried with them as a shared responsibility, turn and turn about. The habit had remained.

No more was said about the five hundred pounds, but that evening Bunbury sat alone in his room, writing a letter of three lines which for that reason required no less than five drafts to perfect its composition—and even then did not thoroughly satisfy the author. When, however, the missive was cobbled together more or less, he put it in a stout manila envelope, together with the five hundred pounds, and sealed the whole thing up with sticky tape.

This done, he addressed the envelope to Ms. Rosalind Purvis at the Walbrook Trust, and went out to post it. Having done that, he felt a whole lot better in himself.

Detective Chief Inspector Ralph Fudge was just about to ring home over a little spot of bother he was having there when the Sawtry complaint was dropped in his lap. As he was duty officer, it was his responsibility, and to his credit he did not pass it further down the line. For one thing, the prospect of a move to Scotland Yard—a decided promotion, and the salary to go with it—had him on his toes. He quizzed the details from Woman Police Sergeant Forrest, who had taken the complaint.

"This Sawtry guy—he is *the* Sawtry?"

"Yes, sir," replied Susan Forrest, who admired Fudge's looks, but despaired of ever getting a human reaction out of him. "The very same. Six wives, and now breaking in his seventh." She regretted the mild vulgarity as soon as it had passed her lips. And she saw him frown slightly: he really was a bit of a prig.

He riffled over the complaint form. " 'Zachary Colenso—U.S. citizen—wife's cousin—missing since around midnight.' This character is well turned twenty-one and quite capable of looking after himself overnight! Why the hell was this complaint accepted, Sergeant? Why didn't you or someone just tell whoever rang up to sit tight for a while and let us know if he doesn't show tomorrow?"

That was another thing, Susan Forrest told herself, he flew off the handle at the slightest thing. "Sir, there's something else about Colenso that alters the case," she said.

"Such as what?" he demanded.

"We have a G-notice on him."

"Do we now?" A G-notice was a preliminary intimation, from the United States Federal Bureau of Investigation, that a known criminal had left the country and was believed to be headed for—was most likely already in—the United Kingdom.

"I've telexed for an amplification on Colenso. It should be here within the half-hour, sir."

He glanced at the clock on the wall, and she saw him do it: ten past six.

"I'll wait till it comes in," said Fudge. "Bring it straight up as soon as it arrives."

"Yes, sir." She went out.

He looked at the phone, which suddenly took on a shape of menace. A quick slug before he got through to home.

The bottle of vodka in the locked bottom drawer of his desk, which Fudge fondly imagined to be a secret from his staff but was, in fact, known to all the subordinates, if not to his superiors—and certainly to Susan Forrest—had to be renewed twice weekly. That, at least, was the fiction he fed himself; every other day was nearer the mark.

He poured three fingers into a shot glass and downed it in one swallow, Slav-fashion—the way he had been taught at that police seminar in Warsaw a couple of years back. The spirit burned him all the way down, fired his faculties, stimulated his courage.

Courageous now, he picked up the phone, asked for an outside line, and dialled home.

"Yes?" came the voice that had always had the power to disturb him.

"Why do you just say 'yes'?" demanded Fudge, and could have bitten off his tongue as soon as the words were spoken. He turned his sharp response into a mild rebuke. "Why not announce the number, like you're supposed to?"

"Oh, I see we're still rowing."

"I'm sorry, I've had a busy day, but—"

"What about me—stuck out here in the lousy sticks in this lousy little rabbit hutch? Or do you have the monopoly of feelings? What time will you be home?"

"I shall be late, I'm afraid. That's really what I'm ringing you about."

"Not again! Can't they run that bloody police station without you once in a while? Or are you on call right round the clock? If so, you're doing it for a slave rate and should go on strike!"

"It's just a routine thing that's cropped up," said Fudge, fighting to keep his patience. "Look, I'll be back as soon as I can, and we'll go out for a late-night supper. How's that?"

"You come any time after seven-thirty and you'll find me out" was the cold response from the other end of the line. "I'm going to put on plenty of slap and get me off down to the club."

"No!" Fudge watched the reflection of his own ravaged expression in the wall mirror opposite his desk. "Don't go without me. Wait till I get back—*please!*"

"Scared that I shall get picked up?"

Fudge closed his eyes. "Yes," he said.

"Well then, that will act as a spur to get you home early, won't it? You can shovel this routine job onto one of your underlings. That whey-faced cow Forrest, who's so keen on you. She'll work through the night for a smile from handsome Ralphie Fudge." The voice, which had become sneeringly mocking, hardened again. "I'll give you till eight o'clock. If you're not back before then, I'm off down to the club, and if some groovy guy picks me up, well—hooray!"

Fudge realized he was sweating badly. If the G-notice amplification was hot, he had no option but to see it right through —and that could mean an all-night sitting. Then it came to him: the trump card that he had kept back, to play when it was a certain winner. How typical that his screwed-up, agonized guts should have conspired to drive it right out of his mind. It was always the same when they were rowing.

"Listen," he said. "I've got great news."

"I'm still here."

"The move to Scotland Yard, and the promotion and a salary boost that goes with it—I've as good as got it. The acting D.C. dropped me the hint this afternoon."

"Ralph! *Dah-ling!*" The voice at the other end rose to a fluting shrillness. "How wonderful! Now we'll be able to move out of this lower-middle-class dump and find us a smart little town house in Camden or Islington where we won't be ashamed to entertain our friends. You're not kidding me, are you, Ralph? You wouldn't put one over on me just to stop me going down to the club on my own?"

"I've as good as got the job," he said. "The acting D.C. spelt it out plain. All I have to do is keep my nose clean till I'm called for a purely routine interview."

"Well, that shouldn't be too difficult. Not for you, darling. Well, you can tell me all about it when you get home. Yes, I'll be waiting for you, don't worry. Wouldn't I do anything, wait any length of time, for a guy who'd take me out of this hell-hole of a district I was brought up in?"

The amplification, when it came, was fairly tame stuff (Fudge had conditioned himself, during the wait, to prejudge it as tame stuff if it showed the slightest sign of being so), but he read it through twice just to make sure.

"This is nothing to get worked up about, Sergeant," he told Susan Forrest. "What we have here is a small-time night-club owner who peddled in prostitution and tried a bit of bigamy on the side. He went through a form of marriage with a rich widow in Kansas City and got away with ten thousand dollars of her savings, which he afterwards blew on getting himself sprung from the penitentiary where he'd been sent on a drugs charge that was probably a frame-up anyhow."

"Mr. Sawtry's adamant that he's been kidnapped," said Susan Forrest. "And he's also worried that his wife will be the next victim. They're leaving for New York tomorrow and he wants a full-blown police escort to follow the convoy of transport he's taking to Heathrow."

Fudge shoved the amplification print-out to one side. "Well, he can whistle for that," he said. "Fix for a single unmarked car to follow this—ah—convoy."

"Yes, sir. Only . . ."

"Only *what*, Sergeant?" He looked up at her sharply, with the sudden cunning of the semi-drunk.

"Nothing, sir." She went out.

Useless to argue with him when he was in that mood. Useless to try and point out that, though the Colenso character was a nobody, Sawtry was one of the ten richest men in the world—and money talks loudly enough to upset the applecarts of lesser persons than Detective Chief Inspector Ralph Fudge.

But the pity of it was, his mind was too full of the need to hurry on down to the southern suburbs—and that awful boyfriend.

NINE

Hugh Ponsonby Greene-ffolks was normally driven to his office in Marsham Street from his home in Chelsea. This particular morning, however, he approached his place of work along Kensington Gore, having spent the night with a friend in South Kensington. Furthermore, for a senior civil servant, Greene-ffolks was unconscionably early—it being only eight-thirty as his taxi carried him along Kensington High Street; this was because his friend had rather nosy neighbours and she made it a condition of their occasional assignations at her place that he was off the premises well before anyone was up and about.

And that was why Hugh Ponsonby Greene-ffolks happened to drive past the Albert Memorial and observe that it was draped from top to bottom with plastic sheeting and bore a notice intimating that it was being washed down by Messrs. Duckworth, Todd & Company.

"Well, I'll be damned!" was Greene-ffolks's reaction to that.

First in his office that morning, and very nearly the first civil servant at his desk in all London, this fairly high-powered executive officer had to wait—seething—till nearly ten o'clock before he was able to contact someone in the Ancient Monuments and Historic Buildings Directorate who was able to meet his wavelength.

He announced himself and his appointment, which was something very high up in the Department of the Environment.

"I'm Pringle, of Monuments Upkeep," responded his putative communicant. "Good morning, sir."

"Now see here!" said Greene-ffolks, ignoring the civility.

"Who in the hell authorized the washing down of the Albert Memorial, and why was I not informed?"

Pringle was perplexed, and said so. He referred to a file and came back with the answer that the Albert Memorial was not due for cleaning till the normal effluxion of time demanded it, and that would be some ten years hence.

"Clearly, there is something amiss in your department," observed Greene-ffolks in the kind of voice and turn of phrase that a junior civil servant does not like to hear from one his senior by at least half a dozen grades. "You had better attend to the issue of the unauthorized cleaning and report back to me in writing, copy to your immediate superior at the AM&HBD."

"Yes, sir. I'll do it right away. An on-site inspection and enquiry," breathed the unhappy young functionary.

It was a beautiful morning: the sort that suggests the kicking off of shoes and dancing barefoot in clover. Young Pringle, when he came to Kensington Gardens, was immune to the charm of summer with all its overtones of secret delights; but then, he had not partaken of the fleshly advantages lately enjoyed by Hugh Ponsonby Greene-ffolks. (And for all that it had benefited the latter in this respect, he might just as well have stayed at home with his spinster sister and their pug dog.

Lacking inner joy, and motivated only by anxiety, Pringle, approaching the memorial on foot by way of the Flower Walk, saw the spire ahead through the trees, and his heart sank upon his observing that the report was correct: the wretched thing was scaffolded, enveloped in plastic sheeting, and undoubtedly in the process of being washed down!

It had only just struck nine-fifteen. There was no sound of running water, no tell-tale torrent pouring from under the sheeting: clearly the workmen had not yet arrived on site. Pringle passed down the eastern side of the vast pyramid that was draped in the plastic from the tip of the spire to the wrought-iron railings surrounding all.

No one was in sight as, passing through a gap in the sheeting on the southern side, he mounted the steps in the cloying heat of the vaulted interior—and came upon a tall man in a light-weight summer suit and a panama hat, who regarded him quizzically from the top step.

"Good morning to you," said the stranger.

"Might I ask what you're doing here?" demanded Pringle, who was in no mood for empty civilities. "This is Crown property."

"Ah, then what are *you* doing here?" countered the other.

"I am from the Ancient Monuments and Historic Buildings Directorate," replied Pringle. "Are you by any chance connected with what's going on here? If so, I . . .

"Good God!" he exclaimed.

His attention—his whole attention, now, the stranger forgotten—was directed to the *America* group: its figures now defaced, the plinth vandalized, and a massive, two-handed saw leaning ominously against the buffalo that bore upon its back the gesticulating figure of America herself.

The first shock having subsided, he spun on his heel and confronted the stranger again.

"Is this—this *outrage*—your work?" he cried.

The other did not reply; instead, he stepped forward the three paces that separated them, made as if to brush a speck of lint from the young man's lapel with his left hand, and, when the other's gaze was deflected by this action, sent his bunched right fist crashing to the point of Pringle's jaw.

Rendered instantly unconscious by the blow, Pringle would have toppled like a felled oak had his assailant not caught him and lowered him gently to the flagstones.

And there he peacefully lay: beneath the bronze gaze of Prince Albert and immediately above the late Zachary Colenso, who was just beginning the second day of his eternal sleep.

The new day brought a surprise to Rosalind Purvis, who, since her spat with Hannah, had collaborated in the pursuit of an absurdly complicated armed truce that called for subterfuges like, say, staggering their breakfast arrangements so that one party went out to the kitchen and washed up her cup, saucer, plate, cutlery, and so forth just as the other sat down to table and poured her coffee. And verbal communications were limited to "Good morning," "Hello," and "Good night."

The mail was late that morning. The letters fell on the mat five minutes after Hannah's Mini had roared away up the road to the West End.

Rosalind's attention was immediately drawn to the large manila envelope that was heavily taped, and addressed to her in a strange handwriting. When she slit it open, a shower of banknotes fell out onto the tablecloth.

There was also a brief note:

Dear Miss Purvis,
You will not remember me, but I recently took advantage of your good nature and cheated you out of £2,000. Here is part-repayment. The rest will follow.

No signature. No word of apology: simply the bare bones of a declaration—that and a partial restitution. Of course, to Rosalind Purvis, there was no need of identification; the declaration of cheating was similarly unnecessary.

The gesture was everything.

Weasel Jilkes and his boys had had a busy night. So had the Man. Almost every hour, Weasel was on the phone to his boss with some news item or other, and gradually the picture of George G. Sawtry's intentions was becoming apparent. The fact of his party's departure for New York the following evening in a specially chartered freight plane they discovered by piecing together the various orders that Sawtry and his henchman Tex had given before retiring for the night. Items like: the bill for the whole party was to be presented before departure around 6 P.M. the following evening; the regular driver of the hired Bentley was to be parked outside the hotel at that hour to take them to Heathrow; Mrs. Sawtry's Aston Martin had been garaged indefinitely pending her next visit to London; there was some talk of a "convoy" that was to assemble. Finally—and this was the clincher—a phone call for the multi-millionaire had been publicly paged around the hotel when he was not to be found in his suite. The caller's name was also announced: *"Colonel Abey on the phone for Mr. Sawtry—Mr. Sawtry, please!"*

A thoroughly determined enquiry is rather like throwing a handful of pebbles into a stagnant pool: the ripples spread outwards, mingle, form configurations of their own, so that echoes come back from echoes, and one is left with almost more movement than one can handle. So it was with Weasel Jilkes's nosing around in the Ritz and elsewhere. . . .

He had elicited, already, that this "Colonel Abey" and his associate, "Dr. Judd," had visited Sawtry's suite on at least one occasion, and that the former answered O'Leary's description. Building upon this briefing, the Man's nimble mind made the imaginative leap that had served to lift him out of the East End back streets into his present eminence.

"That Irish bastard survived the hat-pin!" he declared. "Now he's lying low. But tomorrow he'll be around and up to some shenanigans when Sawtry and his party fly off to New York.

"And we'll be ready for him!"

In this appreciation, the Man had also been helped along by a fact that had come welling up from the stews of the underworld immediately after his over-hasty claim to social rehabilitation because of the alleged settling of his score with O'Leary: it was now being murmured around gangland that O'Leary and an accomplice had pulled a multimillion-dollar con on Sawtry for the Albert Memorial.

The trouble with "the Albert Con" (as it came to be known) was that too many of the wrong sort of people—specifically, the drunken "resting" Thespians—were in the know. In fact, the only people who mattered who were *not* in the know were the very people set in authority to look after the memorial; the exceptions being Hugh Ponsonby Greene-ffolks, who, to give him his due, had done the best he could according to his lights;

and young Pringle of the AM&HBD—and he was at present
lying bound and gagged in a remote plantation of bushes in
the heart of Kensington Gardens, and wondering ruefully why
everything always happened to him.

Six twenty-five.

George G. Sawtry slipped the expanding gold bracelet of his
watch over his thickly pelted wrist and beamed at his reflection in the mirror. The summer-weight tweed from Savile
Row suited him fine, likewise the striped shirt with contrasting
white collar, the discreet tie in knitted silk with a pearl stick-
pin, the hand-made two-tone brogues.

"Ready, hon?" he called out.

Desirée had changed her get-up three times since tea, but
had marginally settled for a summery number in raw silk that
would be comfortable on the plane. She was not one for anything that smacked of the casual, and quite often wore a hat.

"Are we on so tight a schedule?" she called back.

"Sweetie, we are being picked up by the colonel and Dr.
Judd," replied Sawtry. "Together with a little souvenir of our
trip to England which they are transporting for us, and which,
by its nature, I have to keep as a surprise for you. And if you're
ready, we'll go."

Tex and his aides, Duke and Chuck, were waiting by the lift
to escort their employer and his consort down to the street and
their waiting Bentley, and by way of enlivening the scene had
accented their Westernness by eschewing the simplicity of
their skin-tight check suits, string-ties, ruffled shirts, and hand-
tooled boots with the Cuban heels for *la grande tenue* of the
genuine Hollywood cowboy: leather chaps and vests, embroi-
dered shirts, brilliant neckerchiefs, studded gun-belts (but, out
of deference to local customs, no six-shooters); and Duke Dakota, who prided himself on his Indian ancestry, wore a top hat
with a beadwork band and an eagle feather.

The party made their triumphant way across the lobby,
through a double row of bowing functionaries from manager
to bellhop, to the Arlington Street door where a sizeable

crowd of expectant rubberneckers awaited them, having been attracted by the convoy of three limousines parked by the kerb, the last one piled high inside with two sets of matching crocodile luggage, one set coloured pink, the other blue.

"Where's the cops?" muttered Sawtry out of the corner of his mouth to Tex Manacle. "You told 'em to provide the works?"

"Sure did, Eagle-eye," confirmed the other.

"I don't see any patrol cars," complained Sawtry.

"They're around, Eagle-eye. Keeping outa sight, like I explained 'em."

"Police helicopters?"

"Patrolling the route, like I ordered."

"You done well, Tex."

"I aim to please, Eagle-eye."

A stir in the crowd—as a large low-level articulated lorry turned a corner and came lumbering into view, slowing down abreast of the three limousines.

"And here's Abey and Judd—dead on time!" cried the multi-millionaire.

O'Leary was at the wheel. He climbed down from the cab, and Bunbury followed him. George G. Sawtry extended both hands to the two men and wrung theirs, slapped their backs, beamed at them.

"Well done, gentlemen, well done!" he purred. "And I see that"—he nodded towards the low-level trailer upon which rested six enormous wooden packing cases—"I see that you got *America* with you." He winked at them. "I'm sorry I got a little rough with you guys, for you certainly delivered the goods right on the line."

The pair of conspirators looked suitably modest.

"Desirée, my love," declared the mark, "I have arranged for this auspicious occasion to pass not unrecorded. To which end, I have obtained the services of a top-flight photographer to take our pictures. My dear, allow me to introduce . . ." and he brought forth a face and a name famed throughout the developed world as a portrayer of Royalties, Presidents, oil sheiks, and movie stars.

"Gather round! Colonel! Dr. Judd! And you, Tex and the others!"

The crowd allowed itself with some reluctance to be elbowed out of the way, permitting the convoy party to pose in front of the three limousines, with the low-loader and its tantalizing burden filling the whole of the background. The great photographer punished his Hasselblad unmercifully, then switched to a Nikon, which he used like a machine pistol till the spool ran out; Desirée he shot from every angle, culminating in swarming halfway up a lamppost. When he was done, he seemed to collapse like a puppet with no strings.

The party took their seats. Tex Manacle usurped the driver of the second Bentley with a jerk of the thumb that brooked no argument.

"Right!" cried George G. Sawtry, Eagle-eye to his friends. "Let 'em roll!" And in the best waggon-master tradition, he swept his hand and arm down Piccadilly. Westwards—towards the promised land of Heathrow.

No ominous smoke-signals rose in the still air above the distant mountains of Chiswick and Osterley Park—but there were Hostiles waiting on the trail! And, save for a bored policeman in a plain car, who followed the waggon train—convoy— till he lost it at the first set of traffic lights, not a lawman in sight!

The order of advance was as follows: in the lead, the low-loader driver by O'Leary, with Bunbury by his side; followed by the first Bentley bearing the mark and his consort, driven by their usual chauffeur; next came the second limousine with Tex at the wheel and its driver cringing low in his seat every time the big cowpuncher jumped a traffic light or ploughed unregarding through a pedestrian crossing; bringing up the rear was the baggage car. And somewhere well out of sight, the exiguous police escort provided by Detective Chief Inspector Ralph Fudge.

By Piccadilly, Park Lane, and Knightsbridge they went, and on along Kensington Gore. The "three clowns," Dickie, Norman, and Hugo, alerted of the time of their passing, were waiting on the steps of the Albert Memorial—and it still shrouded in plastic sheeting. The clowns cheered and waved Guinness bottles, from which they then toasted the enterprise.

Presently the convoy joined the Great West Road, at no time touching the thirty-mile-an-hour speed limit of legal aspiration, so heavy was the late afternoon traffic. Fulham slid past; the riverside of Hammersmith, with tantalizing glimpses down side-streets to racing shells sculling in the glittering tideway.

And then—*Chiswick and the Hostiles!*

"Great Scott!" shouted Bunbury. "What's that lunatic think he's at?"

O'Leary jammed on the brakes and spun the wheel. A huge furniture removal van, which had come from out of a side turning right across their path, was revealed, on second glance, to be driverless—and the cab door hung wide open. Bunbury saw the front end of the looming juggernaut coming straight at them as O'Leary steered right across the road—disregarding oncoming traffic, which had to take to the pavement—and got clear. In the vehicle following, the chauffeur, who knew a good idea when he saw one, followed after. Tex did likewise, but the tail-ender carrying the baggage went into the side of a Royal Mail van when it tried to do the same.

The Bentley containing the cowboys was now in the rear.

Tex scarcely flinched as a .38 pistol bullet zipped through the car, driving neat holes through rear window and windscreen, and drilling Duke Dakota's top hat from back to front on the way.

"Looks like we collected company," observed Tex. "What do you see back thar, boys?"

Coming up at the rear was a big Jaguar with one of the Man's nameless henchmen at the wheel, and Weasel Jilkes hanging out the front passenger window with a pistol. He took aim.

Fired. Missed—the bullet went over the top of the now speeding Bentley and hit a public house sign on the next corner. The real chauffeur, huddled low in the passenger seat beside Tex, entreated the Westerner to stop and put him down.

Another bullet came in through the rear window. Another scored a metallic furrow along the limousine's pristine side. The Hostiles were closing in for the kill. The regular chauffeur started to scream.

"Only one thing fer it, fellers!" gritted Tex. "Hang on to your hats!"

Dodging in and out of the traffic, overtaking everything in sight, totally disregarding traffic lights, pedestrian crossings, jay-walking old ladies, importuning policemen who blew whistles at him—and pursued all the time by flying lead—Tex contrived, in that busy road, to get his speed up to sixty miles an hour; the Jaguar, following fifteen to twenty yards behind, kept pace.

"Here we go, boys!" cried Tex. "This is gonna hurt them more than it hurts us!"

So saying, he drove his foot hard down on the brake. The limousine practically stood on its head, stopping on the proverbial sixpence. The Jaguar—to give the other driver his due —made a good attempt to do likewise, but his thinking process and reaction time occupied three quarters of the distance separating the two cars. The Jaguar slammed into the rear of the Bentley at around forty miles an hour and drove its elegant radiator grille right back into the engine.

The regular chauffeur was curled up on the floor of the Bentley, thumb in his mouth and keening quietly to himself.

"Let's go, fellers!" cried Tex, opening the door and leaping out. His aides instantly and unquestioningly followed his example; raced down the side of the Bentley to where the Jaguar was more or less attached to its rear by a juncture of tangled metal, from which the steam from a squashed radiator rose in the still air.

There were four men in the Jaguar. Weasel Jilkes, in the front, had dropped his pistol in the collision and was groping for it on the carpeted floor when Duke Dakota, wrenching open the passenger door, seized the unfortunate by the scruff of his neck and the seat of his pants. . . .

"Hokahey!" Giving forth with the triumphant war-whoop of his ancestors, he threw Weasel right over the top of the Jaguar.

The nameless driver, a vicious-looking creature with a pencil-thin moustache and a scarred cheek, was made of different stuff from the Weasel; he groped for a gun under his armpit, at the same time driving forward his two splayed forefingers to the eyes of Chuck Dangerfield, who was reaching to drag him out onto the road. Chuck countered the most immediate of these moves by taking the two fingers and breaking them like a turkey's wishbone. He then relieved the screaming hoodlum of his pistol.

Tex was faring well in the rear compartment, where the Man himself grovelled behind another of his nameless functionaries, who countered Tex's advancing hand and arm with a brutal slash of a flick-knife. Tex stared down at the scarlet furrow that had appeared on his forearm and was filled with an ungovernable rage. Reaching in, he picked out the thug, neck and crop, and hurled him, knife and all, across the street— where he fell at the feet of a much surprised policeman as he stepped out of a patrol car with two others.

"You are all under arrest. And you're warned that anything you say may be taken down and used in evidence. Your names . . . ?"

The bland declarations, unsupported by weaponry, might have been sufficient to silence the Man and his companions, but Tex Manacle, who knew the justice of his cause, had objections.

"Hell to that, copper!" he growled. "These goddamned sonsobitches ambushed us with a truck 'way back and then started shootin'. Ain't there no justice in this country?"

"We are aware of what happened, sir," responded the police sergeant in charge. "And you will have ample opportunity to state your side of the case in due course. And now—all of you empty your pockets, please."

By now a considerable crowd had gathered, but they parted to allow a somewhat aged but well-looked-after Rover to pass through. It came to a halt beside the police patrol car and the driver alighted. He was tall, with grey hair and beard, dressed as a City gentleman, but without the hat, brief-case, and umbrella: a shrewd observer would have elicited that they were lying on the back seat of the Rover.

"Sergeant, I should like a word with you," said the newcomer, in a pleasantly inflected baritone, which nevertheless carried a sharp note of authority. *"Privately!"*

"Indeed, sir," was the sergeant's response. "And for what purpose, whoever you might be?"

"As to who I am . . ." The newcomer took from a crocodile-skin wallet a card, which he handed to the other. One glance, and a remarkable change came over the officer of the law.

"Sorry, sir," he said hastily. "Um—shall we get into my car?"

This they did. There then followed—out of earshot, but in full view of all present—a conversation between the grey-bearded stranger and the sergeant in the front seat of the patrol car; it was noticed very forcibly by all how, though the manner and expression of the newcomer changed not one bit, the sergeant's reactions reflected a shifting of mood from the guarded respect that he had showed upon seeing the other's card, to a certain awe that developed into downright reverence towards the close of his companion's peroration. It was a performance that put Tex Manacle in mind of the snake-medicine man who annually visited the little township where he was born. This personage started out every time with a sullenly resentful crowd who remembered full well how he had cheated them in previous years, but stayed to wonder at that silvery tongue—and to buy, buy, and buy again.

When they at last alighted from the patrol car—and the sergeant dashed round to open the passenger door for the grey-bearded stranger—Tex was near enough—just—to overhear the final injunction that the latter murmured in the sergeant's ear.

"So you will release the Americans to catch their plane—the entire secret operation depends upon it. The others—their assailants—see to it that they are charged with everything that applies: shooting with intent to kill, riotous assembly on the Queen's highway, etc."

"Yessir!" responded the other with slavering fulsomeness.

The grey-bearded man turned to Tex.

"Proceed on your way, my good man," he said imperiously.

Beyond Chiswick, the Great West Road debouching into the unstopping and unstoppable tumult of the M4 motorway as it does, what remained of George G. Sawtry's waggon train—convoy—went the rest of its way to the promised land of Heathrow without further harassment. In scarcely no time at all, they were drawing to a halt by the airport buildings and O'Leary had gone to arrange for the off-loading of the crates.

"Are you both all right?" asked Bunbury, putting his head into the rear passenger window of the Bentley. "That was a most disturbing near-accident. I can't imagine how . . ."

"Sir, that was no accident!" barked Sawtry. "That, sir, was a deliberate and premeditated attempt to ambush and kidnap one or all of us! Yes, Desirée, honey, now that we're within a whisker of safety aboard a United States aircraft, it can be told —you can be told—that we've had a narrow escape from the sonsobitches who kidnapped poor Zach and would have done the same to you, hon, if it hadn't been for the intervention of the police, I don't doubt.

"By the way," he continued, looking round, "where are Tex and the boys?"

"And where's my baggage?" wailed Desirée, who had her priorities right.

At that moment, there appeared the second Daimler with Tex again at the wheel, and a rear fender and boot lid trailing disconsolately behind it. The picturesquely garbed Westerner got out and strode purposefully over to check with his employer, who greeted him with an effusion of relief.

"Tex! You made it, thank Gawd! Tell me what happened."

Tex had his own version of what had happened: a mixture of manly modesty and braggadocio in the finest B-movie Western tradition, enlivened by the undoubted evidence of the blood-stained neckerchief bound about his wounded forearm. He had some good words to say for the timely intervention of the police patrol car, and his voice took on a note of awe when he touched upon the grey-bearded stranger and the aura of power which had emanated from him.

"That guy," he said, "I kid you not, Eagle-eye, he was like J. Edgar Hoover and Al Capone rolled into one. When that guy said 'Jump,' they jumped! Believe me, if they were the guys who kidnapped Mr. Colenso, they'll be singing like canaries by tonight, with that bearded guy around."

"Good, good!" said Sawtry. "Ah, here comes Colonel Abey. All fixed with the you-know-what, Colonel?"

"The crates are being loaded aboard the freighter right away, sir," said O'Leary. "You and madame can take your places aboard the freighter any time you choose. The passenger accommodation is, I am told, of the very highest standard."

"What about my baggage?" wailed Desirée. "I can't wear this thing I've got on all through a night flight and arrive in New York looking like I've been selling hot dogs on Coney Island!"

The departure of the Sawtrys and the *America* crates went off without a hitch. The missing limousine and their luggage even turned up on time—towed by a breakdown truck.

Desirée contrived a quiet minute aside with the two conspirators—one might almost say her two *fellow conspirators*—in the VIP lounge, where the party toasted the success of the venture in vintage champagne. Her baggage having arrived, she had managed to change into a zippy little cocktail number for the occasion.

"Boys, I want to say that I appreciate the way you've played ball with me," she declared, "and in return you can be sure that I aim to play ball right back. The five million bucks is yours—right to the end of the line."

"Desirée, you're a doll," said O'Leary.

"A real brick," said Bunbury.

"And we've nothing to worry about," she continued. "George is convinced that Zach was kidnapped by the same gang that tried to ambush us, and he's going to sell that idea solid to the cops on both sides of the Atlantic. No one in his right mind's going to start digging around for poor Zach—the rat!"

The flight was called. Time for farewells. Bunbury and O'Leary kissed her cheek. "I guess we'll never meet again, boys," she said. "You'll be making yourselves scarce with the five—right?"

"Just as soon as we can get a flight out," said O'Leary.

"Well, good luck."

"And you, Desirée," said Bunbury.

They shook hands with Sawtry and the cowboys. Bunbury might have experienced a slight pang of regret about the quite appalling con they had played on the Texan multimillionaire, but compared with the deception he had practised on Rosalind Purvis, it lay upon his conscience like a featherweight, and more than offset by the appalling service they had been obliged to render to Desirée.

With champagne glasses re-charged, they watched the big freighter waddle like a beached turtle across the apron and out onto the end of the runway, lights flashing in the summer's gloaming. The four massive turbo-props whirred madly, a moment's pause as they subsided—and then the great machine rolled forward, gathering speed down the wide path that led westwards to the declining sun.

Bunbury and his comrade raised their glasses, and the toast was "To the five-million-dollar Prince!"

They drained glasses.

"I think we should smash them so they'll never be used

again," said Bunbury. Someone—a total stranger—had entered the lounge and was looking their way. For some reason he felt constrained to lower his voice. "But I think we can spare ourselves that outdated gesture," he added.

His companion had his back turned towards the new arrival, so that he did not see him. On the other hand, Bunbury was admirably well able to observe the effect of the newcomer's stentorian voice upon the countenance of the man he had grown to know and admire as Tom O'Leary. . . .

"*SEVEN-FIVE-SIX-TWO-THREE-THREE GUARDSMAN DONOVAN, P.S.!*"

The barrack-square bellow almost shattered the empty glass in Bunbury's suddenly nerveless hand.

"*SAH!*"

Without turning to check on the origin of the bellow (he knew well enough), the addressee sprang to attention and stared rigidly before him.

The newcomer came forward. Tall as Bunbury's fellow conspirator, dark and blue-eyed and possessing a quite remarkable resemblance to the other so that they might have been brothers, or cousins at least, he also had the same soldierly manner and bearing.

"Stand easy, Donovan," he said.

"Thank you, sir."

"What's going on?" demanded Bunbury. "And who for heaven's sake *is* this chap—and why is he calling you Donovan?"

"Because it's my real name, Horse," said the other. He grinned and indicated the man by his side. "Meet the *real* Captain Tom O'Leary," he said. And to the latter, "How're you keeping, Tom?"

"Well enough, Seamus," came the reply. "And by the way things strike me, I came back to England just in time to pull your chestnuts out of the fire, my lad!"

He smiled fondly at his addressee, and Bunbury took time to

notice that there was a patch of what looked like dried glue on the angle of his jaw, with something adhering to it. Something that might have been a strand of grey whisker. Only, of course, it meant nothing to Bunbury at the time.

TEN

Bunbury, suffering from a sense of total exclusion from the reunion of his two companions, allowed himself to be led to the nearest airport bar, where he accepted a virgin Mary and watched and listened while O'Leary (the *new*, mark-one O'Leary) held the floor—as, Bunbury swiftly discovered, the latter had a habit of doing.

"I hadn't thought to see you again, Seamus," he said, "not, at least, till you had made your packet at the con game, or when, realizing the futility of the struggle, you had come to join me on my Greek island."

"Hell, Tom, how would I ever find that damned island," demanded the other, "since you've never even told me its name!"

"Nor shall I, till you're ready for it, old lad," replied O'Leary. "For it's my secret from all the world, save for the handful of folks who live there—fine people, all, who're like family to me."

"And I suppose they look upon you as a reincarnation of some pagan Greek god fresh down from Parnassus?"

"Something like that," admitted the other. He next addressed himself to their companion. "You should know, Bunbury, that Seamus here was my batman* in the Irish Guards," he said. "Shared with me in everything, including my disgrace and dismissal. We took to crime together, and he showed a considerable talent in that direction—as you will have noticed."

* Batman: In the British Army, a fighting soldier who fights alongside his officer and also acts as his servant, driver, general factotum.

—M.B.

"Masterminded a five-million con for the Albert Memorial," interjected Donovan smugly. "With the invaluable aid of my friend here," he added.

"It was a good con," conceded O'Leary, "but flawed in many regards, and I'll be having more to say about that later."

"Tell me now, Tom," said Donovan, "how did you get on to us? And why did you leave your Greek island in the first place?"

It seemed to Bunbury that O'Leary looked at their companion with some disappointment, as if he had expected more of his ex-batman. "You should have figured that, Seamus," he replied, "remembering, as you do, that poor Walter Tite was in the Guards with us before he went into banking, and was of considerable use to us in our operations when it came to laundering and similar services.

"Walter ran a straight business also, but I had his complete confidence in all his questionable activities. He once said to me, 'Tom, you're the only man in the world I really trust. If anything happens to me, I beg you to come and clear up any messes I may have left behind. Do this for me—for the sake of Anne and the children.'

"Which is why I came to England immediately I heard the news of his suicide on the Overseas Service of the BBC."

"And you tripped over—us," said Donovan.

"I came across the bare details of your five-million con in Walter's secret diary, whose whereabouts he'd confided in me," said O'Leary. "So I set out to find you. The trail didn't lead me far. A couple of days later, I heard on the underworld grape-vine that the Man was claiming to have had O'Leary killed. Even the *modus operandi* was quite specific: stabbing with a hat-pin."

"A hat-pin!" exclaimed Donovan, exchanging glances with Bunbury.

"Zach Colenso!" cried the latter.

"That explains a lot!"

They discussed the implications of the Colenso mix-up and ordered another round of drinks.

Presently O'Leary said, "Accepting that Donovan was dead, Bunbury, it seemed that there were only two things left for me to do—and that was to carry on the vendetta with the Man one stage further by avenging him, and to give you, his last comrade, any help I could. To the latter end, I stayed in the background and helped along where I was able. F'rinstance, when it got around the underworld about your Albert Memorial con, I went along to the memorial and narrowly prevented the Ancient Monuments, or whatever they call themselves, from latching on to what you were about.

"Which reminds me, I must ring them and advise them to pick up that unfortunate young man. . . ."

Donovan sat back in his chair and, eyeing his former officer and sometime partner in crime quizzically, he put the question: "Tell me straight, Tom. Speaking as the guy who taught me all I know about the con game as you practised it—the typography and printing, the forging of official papers, all that and more—what's your honest opinion of our Albert Memorial job?"

"Seamus," said the other, "when I heard about it, I was consumed with pride and admiration—and still am. The general plan, the execution, the pay-off—all these were beautifully carried out, and a credit to me—your master." He paused.

"But . . . ?" interposed Donovan, grave-faced.

"Your talents are great, Seamus," continued the other. "And in Bunbury, here, you found the perfect foil—the Dr. Watson to your Sherlock Holmes. Just as I was the sorcerer and you the sorcerer's apprentice in the old days. But, like the sorcerer's apprentice, the job was too big for you. The first snag that came along and you were out of your depth. Right up to the time you collected the mark's cheque, you never put a foot wrong, but after that—phiuu!" He turned to address Bunbury. "In the old days, I always handled the high finance, you see? Donovan never even got the hang of double-entry bookkeeping, let alone how to make millions disappear at the laundry. The only hope you two had was my connection with Walter Tite. When the Board of Trade started pressuring him that night and he killed himself, you ran right out of luck. And the transport strike was the last nail in the coffin of your hopes."

He smiled broadly. "I owe my old batman a lot, Bunbury. At my wish, he took over my name, reputation, and operations here—along with the cabin trunk containing all my working gear—so that I could fade out of the scene on my Greek island. For covering up my tracks, I'd do a lot for him." He grinned at the man in question.

"Would you launder that five-million cheque, Tom?" asked Donovan.

"I thought you'd never ask," replied O'Leary. "Yes, I'll do it —for the usual 20 per cent commission."

"Done!" cried Donovan. "Give the gentleman the cheque, Horse!"

Bunbury groped in his breast pocket for his wallet. He looked slightly miffed not to find it there; but persevered and tried his hip pocket, then his trousers, his side pockets, everywhere.

By then, his companions were staring at him in a concerted amalgam of horror and disbelief.

"Don't tell me . . ." began Donovan.

"It—it's gone!" breathed Bunbury. "I remember now. Outside the Ritz, when we were posing for our photos. Someone in the crowd jostled me. . . ."

"You've been dipped!" said Donovan.

"It's gone," said Donovan presently, and with more equanimity than one would have given him credit for. "And whoever's got it . . ."

"Whoever dipped for that wallet and found a cheque for five million bucks inside it," said O'Leary, "if he, or she, had half a grain of common sense—would take it for some kind of party joke and throw it on the fire. Was there any money in the wallet, Bunbury?"

"About ten pounds," supplied the latter gloomily.

"In that case the dip would ditch the joke cheque with a laugh and consider he'd made a good haul."

"He might try banking it," suggested Bunbury.

"In which case he's sitting in some cop-shop by now, not answering a lot of questions."

They called for another round of drinks.

"You were on very good terms with Mrs. Sawtry, surely, after you disposed of her unwanted husband's corpse," said O'Leary, who had heard this part of the story, of course. "Couldn't you touch her for a replacement cheque?"

"She has a private account, I don't doubt," said Donovan, "like she can pick up the phone and have a nearly new Aston Martin delivered at her door. But even her fond George G. might ask questions about the odd cheque for five million."

"What percentage, then, in taking the bull by the horns and trying Sawtry himself?"

"Tom, we might have tried that half an hour ago before he got onto that plane," replied Donovan. "And he might have come across. But after he gets into New York, the names of Abey and Judd are going to be like poison in his mouth. And not even your silver tongue would persuade him otherwise.

"Right, Horse?"

"Right!" endorsed Bunbury. "Not a hope!"

The slowish freight plane reached JFK in the early hours of the morning, and the alarums and excursions of the previous day had so overstimulated Sawtry and his beautiful consort that they had hardly slept during the flight; on their arrival, therefore, both were in tetchy mood and had already had a spat over breakfast. There was also a delay in landing; half an hour in the stack, with visions of their comfortable East Side duplex down there below, with a warm bath, decent coffee, and comfortable beds, was enough to put them both—but George G. Sawtry particularly—in truculent and trouble-seeking mood. The essential of multimillionaires is that, like rattlesnakes and other fundamentally beneficent beings with a built-in potency, they can afford to be all sweetness and light—till someone treads on their tail.

By the time they alighted from the plane, Desirée had, by an injudicious piece of nagging, fired Sawtry's temper to dangerous heights, thereby precipitating a situation without which the saga of the Albert Con would certainly have had a very different ending.

Ill chance, moreover, compounded the issue further by ordaining that there should be a customs shake-up at JFK on account of a large consignment of narcotics that had slipped through the previous day and had only been seized later through the astuteness of the common or garden New York police. Much miffed by this, the U.S. Customs and the Drug Enforcement Administration were very much on their toes to prevent any further slip-ups—at least till the last one was safely buried and forgotten.

Fate had dealt the cards from the bottom of the deck; the last hand was about to be played out. . . .

"Mr. George G. Sawtry to the freight shed for Customs clearance!" The announcement came over the public address system just as the multimillionaire was presenting his and Desirée's passports.

"This is a load of crap!" growled he. "Tex Manacle and the boys can deal with that!"

But the powers that be were adamant. Sawtry was conducted to the freight shed and his six enormous crates were pointed out to him.

"The manifest says there's a statuary group in there," scowled an official, pointing.

"That's what it says—and that's what it is!" responded Sawtry.

"Open it up!" ordered the other of his minions.

"Like hell you will!" bawled Sawtry. "Do you know who I am?"

"The hell I don't—or care! The manifest says the consignment weighs ten tons plus. That could be ten tons plus of heroin and cocaine for all I know!"

"Damn you! Lay a hand on one of those crates and you and your wife and your goddamned kids will starve!" shouted Sawtry.

"George," murmured Desirée placatingly. "Let be! They're only hunks of old stone."

It was her diplomacy and physical configuration which sufficiently softened the resolve of the functionary so that he agreed to summon his superior to make the judgement as to whether the crates should be opened or not.

A messenger was dispatched to fetch the oracle; Sawtry flopped down heavily in a seat and mopped his brow.

"That guy," he panted, "was just a flak-catcher. The big shot will know me for whom I am. Connections with the White House. Congress. Wall Street.

"That was a great move of yours—to soften up the bastard."

His laugh expired in a choking cough. He died with a rictus grin on his face, without seeing inside the six crates. Still reeking of his appalling Old Chaps after-shave.

The big shot came. Despite the death of the owner (or perhaps the more so), the six containers were all opened—to disclose ten tons plus of broken stone and rubble, as supplied by the contractor who had loaded up the crates.

This provided no great surprise to Desirée, but brought some muttered comment from the customs officials.

"If this is what they call modern sculpture, I've seen everything!"

"A helluva load of junk to get dead about!"

It was on the eve of the Man's trial at the Old Bailey on miscellaneous charges connected with the shooting affray in the Great West Road that Mrs. Desirée Sawtry [*sic*] arrived back in England and was fêted by the popular press, interviewed on TV, and generally celebrated in the phrase dreamed up by one of the satirical weeklies: "The World's Most Eligible Widow." Her beauty, wealth, charm, and so forth, were of such a high order that fame was inescapable;

what added a twist of piquancy was the sixfold lawsuit filed against her in the New York courts for shares in the multimillion legacy that George G. Sawtry's six former wives and their expensive lawyers considered (and with more justification than they knew!) to be theirs *a fortiori.*

Upon her arrival, she had her own lawyers seek out the pair whom she still only knew by the sobriquets of Abey and Judd, Colonel and Doctor of Philosophy respectively; this was not easy, for the former was unemployed, drawing a hand-out from the State and dreaming of another such Albert Con as would change his life again; Bunbury had simply gone back to being a tour guide in London—though not in the employ of Scott & Lloyds, even if they would have had him back; the thought of showing tourists the Albert Memorial was more than his flesh and blood could contemplate to bear.

Eventually, however, and after much expense, the determined little widow ran the pair of them to earth and invited them to meet her for dinner at the Ritz—*à trois,* she stipulated, in her private suite. Nothing loath, for neither was greatly encumbered with social engagements, the two of them met up for a drink to put them in the mood (Bunbury had relapsed after the shock of the Albert Con fiasco but had got it well under control still—he told himself), they presented themselves at Desirée's suite and found her not greatly changed: still almost too beautiful for belief, dressed simply in mourning black, a glass of Martini by her elbow.

Mutual compliments were exchanged. Something about her manner—the way she bit her quite perfect nether lip, a straying of the eyes when the conversation flagged, the tapping of her impeccably manicured forefinger on the chair arm—suggested to Bunbury that she was under some strain. Prompted, she told them that George G. had been interred at one of the modern memorial parks in his home state, and that she had commissioned a prominent Italian sculptor to carve an heroic-sized portrait figure of the little Texan in the pose of shielding his eyes from the sun and gazing out over his almost illimitable acres—this to stand in the Hall of Achievement at the memorial park.

Over dinner, served in her drawing-room by half a dozen soft-footed waiters, Desirée played the perfect hostess: pressing them to extra portions of steak Chateaubriand, bidding them to recharge their glasses with the priceless Burgundy while confining herself to Martinis and slimming biscuits. She had also put on dark glasses, and the sensitive Bunbury opined to himself that she was crying.

The dessert, cheeses, and fruit having been cleared away, the two men toyed with suave liqueurs and waited their hostess's pleasure regarding the true reason for the dinner invitation, for even with the best will in the world, it seemed hardly likely that their recent assistance in the disposal of her late husband's corpse was cause for a reunion party.

She came out with it after her fifth Martini—the fifth of their witnessing. "Boys," she began, "I am in one helluva fix!"

The two men exchanged glances and made sympathetic noises.

"Those six bitches"—Desirée named the former wives of George G. Sawtry, and they were an assortment of most extraordinarily heterogeneous origins: two ex-movie actresses, a former college professor, an Olympic gold-medallist, a numismatist of distinction, and a torch singer; all of them multidivorcées—"those six bitches are after George's money—*my* money!

"My attorney says they haven't a hope, on account of they all signed deeds agreeing to fixed annuities for life and not to upset these agreements. But they've all gotten into the hands of shark lawyers who aim to collect on a fifty-fifty basis. It's going to be a hard fight, and it's going to cost me to contest the claims through the courts. But, like my attorney says, I'm 99 per cent certain to win. Only . . ."

Seamus Donovan, yclept O'Leary, supplied the answer for all three of them: "Only you were never married to George G. Sawtry, were you, Desirée? So you've really no claim on his estate. No claim at all."

"I checked out," she said, "when details of George's liquidity were sent to me from the bank, that you boys still haven't cashed in that cheque for five million."

Both nodded assent, but said nothing.

"It occurred to me," she continued, "that maybe on account of the size of the amount, plus the odd circumstances of your obtaining same, you had encountered some difficulty in liquidizing the cheque."

"We did worse than that, Desirée," said Donovan. "We lost it."

"I lost it," said Bunbury.

A little time went by. Desirée ran a slender forefinger down her Martini glass and remarked how it left a clear trail through the slight condensation. "There are no records of my marriage to Zach Colenso," she said. "The drunken notary who said a few words over us is long dead. Only you two guys could testify that I married George bigamously. You—and Zach lying out there under the monument where you buried him."

"I think we have a deal," said Donovan. "What do you say, Horse?"

"Undoubtedly," responded Bunbury.

"What do you have in mind?" asked Desirée warily.

"A replacement cheque for the five million?" Donovan cocked an interrogative eye at his companion, who nodded in reply.

Desirée looked relieved. "That sounds a very fair deal, boys," she said.

"Made out to cash," said Donovan.

"And a special arrangement with your bank's branch or stringer in London," added Bunbury, remembering all the snags, "whereby we can collect immediately and without question."

"If necessary in cash," added Donovan. "We don't have any talent for the ins-and-outs of high finance."

"I'll fix it right away," said Desirée. "And I think this calls for champagne."

They toasted each other. Absent friends. The Albert Memorial. And Desirée added, "You know what? —I shall always feel that I share the Albert Memorial with Queen Victoria."

It was a nice, sensitive touch.

The afternoon carried heavy overtones of impermanency; the look of a rose on the way to being overblown conveys the same mood. The trees in Hyde Park were of the deepest possible green and some of them were already threatening russet-brown. It was one of the last of the languid days of a perfect summer, the like of which reminds one of the end of youth, the closing of an era.

The music of a military band drifted through the trees, and children were laughing down by the lake, when Horace Bunbury went to keep his tryst with a fate that was no more substantial than a shadow cast upon a blind, a whisper in the dark; to him it held the promise and the permanency of a rock set on a high hill.

There were a few tables left in the outdoor café. He selected one that was half in shadow, half in shade, and sat down to wait.

"Was you wanting tea, sir?" A little waitress quizzed him.

"Yes, please. For two. With cucumber sandwiches and cream-cakes."

"For two?"

"My friend hasn't come yet."

"Shall you wait till . . . ?"

"Bring it now. She'll be here any minute."

Such assurance. But he never questioned the certainty. And when he saw her turn into the garden and look about her, it was as if they had been meeting every day of their lives. The sudden familiarity, when he got up and took her proffered hand, was all of a piece with the gentle ease with which he enquired how she was and how she had a marvellous tan.

"Yes, I've been to Greece," she said. "With Hannah—she was the friend you met when we were last here."

"Oh yes." He remembered Hannah. And a light cloud passed overhead.

The waitress came with a laden tray, and the ritual of pouring and helping provided a bridge to span the slight constraint that had seemed to separate them. Bunbury had framed the words which would introduce the topic that lay uppermost in his mind and must surely do in hers; he was struggling to recall the exact turn of phrase that had seemed so apposite when he had tried it out the night before, when she came out with an introduction that was quite unequivocal.

"I got your cheque for fifteen hundred pounds this morning. Thanks so much."

"Did it come first or second post?" he heard himself ask.

"First." She appeared unconscionably pleased to be offered the opportunity of a banal answer.

"I only wondered because I posted the letter after six, and one can't rely on them arriving first thing unless one posts before midday."

"Yes, the mail is very uncertain this time of the year. Like at Christmas. I suppose because people are on holiday."

"Do you know," he said, "I think it's going to rain."

"I do believe you're right. It's clouding over. Dark as pitch over there." She pointed.

Their eyes met, and she still posed with her hand and finger pointing.

"I don't think a day has passed," he said, "when I haven't regretted the way I cheated you. You know it wasn't my roof, or my house, don't you?"

"Yes. Hannah drew my attention to the advertisement."

"Oh—Hannah."

"She didn't like you from the first," said Rosalind. "Said you were shifty and a wrong 'un."

"In the circumstances," he said, "she was right. What did she think about your meeting me for tea today?"

"She doesn't know. We don't share house any more. She fell in love with someone and ran off with him."

"You look disapproving," he said.

"I thought he was shifty from the first," she said. "And I was right. He turned out to be already married." She laughed. "Are you already married, Mr. Bunbury?"

"No," he said, adding, "Do you believe me?"

"Yes," she said.

"Why—do you believe me?"

"Because I know that you will never lie to me again."

("Because I know that you will never lie to me again." —And, surely, thought Bunbury, those are some of the loveliest words that were ever strung together.)

"It's raining," said Rosalind. "I felt a spot on my hand. Look —there it is."

The better to inspect the spot of rain, he took her hand; nor did he relinquish it.

"You don't really claim grants you're not entitled to for a living, do you?" she asked. "I mean—that was just a once-and-for-all-time aberration, wasn't it?"

"Yes."

"Do you mind if I ask what you really do for a living?"

"I'm a millionaire," he said. "A dollar millionaire."

"A dollar millionaire." She nodded gravely. "Yes, that would explain everything. Not only a millionaire, but you're also an eccentric. They often go together, so I've heard."

"I really should explain . . ." began Bunbury; but she laid the fingers of her free hand gently upon his lips.

"No, that would spoil everything," she said. "The way it is leaves so much room for speculation."

A distant flash of lightning followed by a drum-roll of thunder heralded a sudden shower of rain. People left their tables outside and ran into the café; but Bunbury and his Rosalind stayed where they were and braved the downpour under their sheltering tree.

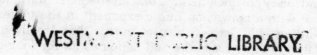

ENVOI

Unknowingly anticipating Tom O'Leary's telephone call, a courting couple who entered the remote plantation of bushes in Kensington Gardens for reasons that were no one's business but their own found young Pringle of the AM&HBD and set him free. The following morning he led a party of officials accompanied by police and took a symbolic repossession of the violated Albert Memorial, where, apart from the scaffolding and plastic sheeting that still remained, they found everything in apple-pie order; the three clowns had made good the spurious work they had put in on the *America* plinth, and the noble figures thereon had been washed clean of Bunbury's deceitful dotted lines. The cheerful Thespians themselves were propped up against Prince Albert's podium and sleeping off the effects of bottled Guinness, the "empties" having been neatly replaced in their crates after use. Brought up before the Bow Street magistrate that same morning on a charge of trespass on Crown property, Dickie, Norman, and Hugo were given an unconditional discharge and departed rejoicing on the dot of pub opening time.

The rain that is sent upon the just and the unjust alike fell capriciously upon Detective Chief Inspector Ralph Fudge, who was rightly held responsible for failing to provide an escort that could have prevented the shooting affray in the Great West Road, and he did not get his anticipated promotion and salary advancement, so that his friend left him and went to live with a rising pop music exponent in the better part of Notting Hill Gate—a turn of events that greatly improved Ralph Fudge's social life and happiness in the long run.

The rain fell quite unequivocally upon the Man and his

henchmen. Darkie Todd, judged by a Bristol post-mortem to have died of a coronary, was safe from all earthly reckoning in a pauper's grave; not so the others. With records such as theirs, going back through uncounted years of crime, they were lucky to escape life sentences for causing an armed affray on the Queen's highway. In fact, they all received stiff terms of imprisonment, to be spent—as if to make the Man's cup of bitterness overflow—in the Scrubs.

Far from London and Kensington Gore, Seamus Donovan, sometime known as O'Leary, lives out an idyllic existence on the secret Greek island where he has joined his former officer and late accomplice in crime.

Every year without fail, they are visited by Horace and Rosalind Bunbury in their yacht *Albertina;* and in the velvet nights of the Aegean, with the whisper of sentinel cypresses all round them and the sound of bouzoukis coming up from the beach, they sit around a campfire and drink retsina; and Rosalind listens, bemused and uncomprehending, while the menfolk talk of their friend Albert, and the good fortune he has so generously brought their way.

ABOUT THE AUTHOR

Michael Butterworth has gained an enthusiastic following for his masterful suspense novels, including *A Virgin on the Rocks, X Marks the Spot,* and *The Man Who Broke the Bank at Monte Carlo.* He lives in Wiltshire, England.